Hugo ... *Alice* ... *one of* ... *a bright iridescent blue, flapped lazily over to them, then landed on his arm.*

His eyes were full of wonder; all the cynicism had gone from his face. At that moment, it felt as if he lit up the whole butterfly house for her. It was the sweetest, sweetest feeling. As if they were sharing something special. Something private. Their own little world.

"You can breathe, you know," she said softly. "You won't hurt it."

"That's just..." He shook his head, clearly lost for words.

She couldn't resist standing on tiptoe and brushing her mouth against his.

He froze for a moment, and then, as the morpho flew away again, he wrapped his arms around her waist, returning the kiss. She slid her arms around his shoulders, drawing him closer. And then he really kissed her. All around them, butterflies flapped their iridescent wings, and she closed her eyes, letting all her senses focus on the feel of Hugo's mouth against hers.

Dear Reader,

I'm thrilled that this is my ninetieth book for Harlequin!

I wanted to do something a little different and play with one of the tropes I remember reading avidly when I was in my teens: the will with a Very Big Condition. Hugo and Alice are perfect for each other, but both refuse to date. Rosemary uses her will to get them together. And, although they loathe each other on first sight, they discover that they are perfect to help the other move on from the past.

With Alice being a butterfly specialist and Hugo being an architect, I thoroughly enjoyed researching for this book—visiting gorgeous glass domes (especially the Reichstag in Berlin), butterfly houses (London, with my best friend) and sites of special scientific interest (I took my husband to the hill fort where Hugo and Alice see the blue butterflies, and the look of wonder on his face when he realized I hadn't been teasing...that was definitely a romantic moment!).

I hope you enjoy their journey.

With love,

Kate Hardy

A Will, a Wish, a Wedding

—

Kate Hardy

Recycling programs
for this product may
not exist in your area.

ISBN-13: 978-1-335-55645-5

A Will, a Wish, a Wedding

Copyright © 2020 by Pamela Brooks

Harlequin Enterprises ULC
22 Adelaide St. West, 40th Floor
Toronto, Ontario M5H 4E3, Canada
www.Harlequin.com

Printed in U.S.A.

Kate Hardy has been a bookworm since she was a toddler. When she isn't writing, Kate enjoys reading, theater, live music, ballet and the gym. She lives with her husband, student children and their spaniel in Norwich, England. You can contact her via her website: katehardy.com.

Books by Kate Hardy

Harlequin Romance

Visit the Author Profile page at Harlequin.com for more titles.

To Gerard, Chris and Chloe, who've supported me
all the way through ninety books, with all my love.

Praise for
Kate Hardy

"Ms. Hardy has written a very sweet novel about
forgiveness and breaking the molds we place
ourselves in... A good heartstring novel that will
have you embracing happiness in your heart."

—*Harlequin Junkie* on *Christmas Bride for the Boss*

CHAPTER ONE

YOU DON'T BELONG HERE, oik, a posh voice sneered in Alice's head.

Barney and his cronies would've laughed themselves sick if they could've seen her standing at the foot of a set of white marble steps. What business did the girl from the council estate have here, in the poshest bit of Chelsea?

She lifted her chin to tell the voice she wasn't listening. Ten years ago, she'd been so naive that she hadn't realised that Barney—the most gorgeous man at the Oxford college where they were both studying—was only dating her for a bet. She'd found out the truth at the college ball where she'd thought he was going to propose, while he'd been planning to collect his winnings after proving he'd turned the oik into a posh girl. He hadn't loved her for herself or even wanted her; instead, it had been a warped kind of Eliza Doolittle thing. He and his friends had been laughing at her all along, and she'd been so hurt and ashamed.

Now Dr Alice Walters was a respected lepidopterist. She was comfortable with who she

was professionally and was happy to give keynote speeches at high-powered conferences; but
socially she always had to silence the voice in her
head telling her that she wasn't good enough—
especially if her surroundings were posh.

Why *had* Rosemary Grey's solicitor asked to
see her? Maybe Rosemary had left some specimens to the university. Or maybe this was about
the project they'd worked on together: editing the
journals and writing the biography of the butterfly collector Viola Ferrers, Rosemary's great-
grandmother. Alice had visited her elderly friend
in hospital several times after her stroke and, although Rosemary's sentences had been jumbled,
her anxiety had been clear. Alice had promised
Rosemary that she'd see the project through.
Hopefully, whoever had inherited the journals
would give her access to them, but she needed to
be in full professional mode in case there were
any doubts. Now really wasn't the time for im-
poster syndrome to resurface and point out that
she looked a bit awkward in the business suit and
heels she hardly ever wore, there was a bit of hair
she hadn't straightened properly, and her make-
up wasn't sophisticated enough.

The one thing Barney's callousness had taught
her all those years ago was that image *mattered*—
even though she thought people should judge her
by what was in her head and her heart, not by

what she looked like. For now she'd go with the superficial and let them judge the butterfly by its chrysalis.

'This is for you and Viola, Rosemary,' Alice said softly. She walked up the steps to the intimidatingly wide front door with its highly polished brass fittings and pushed it open.

'May I help you?' the receptionist asked.

Alice gave her a very professional smile. 'Thank you. I'm Dr Alice Walters. I have an appointment with Mr Hemingford at two-thirty.'

The receptionist checked the screen and nodded. 'I'll let him know you're here, Dr Walters. The waiting area's just through there. Can I offer you a cup of coffee while you're waiting?'

Alice would have loved some coffee, but she didn't want to risk spilling it all over her suit—and right now she was feeling nervous enough to be clumsy. 'Thank you for the offer, but I'm fine,' she said politely, and headed for the waiting area.

There were a couple of others sitting there: a middle-aged woman who kept glancing at her watch and frowning, as if her appointment was running a bit late, and a man with floppy dark hair and the most amazing cobalt-blue eyes who was staring out of the window, looking completely lost.

For one crazy moment, she thought about going over to him and asking if he was all right.

She knew from working with her students that if someone was having a rough day, human contact and a bit of kindness could make all the difference.

But the man was a stranger, this was a solicitor's office, and whatever was wrong was none of her business. Besides, she needed to make sure she was prepared for anything, given the infuriating vagueness of the solicitor's letter. So she sat down in a quiet corner, took her phone from her bag, and re-read the notes she'd made about the butterfly project.

Hugo Grey still couldn't quite believe that his eccentric great-aunt was dead. He'd thought that Rosemary would live for ever. She'd been the only one of his family he could bear to be around when his life had imploded nearly three years ago. Unlike just about everyone else in his life, she hadn't insisted over and over that he shouldn't blame himself for Emma's death, or tried to make him talk about his feelings; she'd simply asked him to come and help her with an errand that almost always didn't materialise, made him endless cups of tea and given him space to breathe. And there, in that little corner of Notting Hill, he'd started to heal and learn to face the world again.

He'd spent the first three months of this year in Scotland, so he hadn't been able to visit Rosemary as much as he would've liked, but he'd still called her twice a week and organised a cleaner and a weekly grocery delivery for her. Once he was back in London, he'd popped in on Monday and Thursday evenings, and she'd been fine—until the stroke. He'd visited her in hospital every other day, but it had been clear she wouldn't recover.

And now he was to be her executor.

Just as he'd been for Emma. Hugo knew exactly how to register a death, organise a funeral, plan a wake, write a good eulogy and execute a will, because he'd already done it all for his wife.

He clenched his fists. He'd let Emma down—attending an architectural conference thousands of miles away in America instead of being at her side when she'd had that fatal asthma attack. If he'd been home, in London, he could've got medical help to her in time to save her. He couldn't change the past, but he could learn from it; he wasn't going to let his great-aunt down. She'd trusted him to be her executor, so he'd do it—and he'd do it *properly*.

He glanced round the waiting room. There were two others sitting on the leather chairs: a middle-aged woman who was clearly impatient at being kept waiting, and a woman of around his own age who looked terrifyingly polished.

It was nearly half-past two. Thankfully Philip Hemingford was usually punctual. Hugo could hand over the death certificate, and then start working through whatever Rosemary wanted him to do. He knew from the copy of the will she'd given him that she'd left nearly everything to his father and there were some smaller bequests; he'd make sure everything was carried out properly, because he'd loved his eccentric great-aunt dearly.

A door opened and Hugo's family solicitor appeared. 'Mr Grey, Dr Walters?'

Dr Walters?

Hugo had been pretty sure this appointment was for him alone; he was representing his father, who wasn't well. Who on earth was Dr Walters?

The terrifyingly polished woman stood up, surprising him. She didn't look like the sort of person who'd pop in to see Rosemary for a cup of tea and a chat. Hugo knew all Rosemary's neighbours, and his great-aunt hadn't mentioned anyone moving into the street recently. This didn't feel quite right.

'Please, have a seat,' Philip Hemingford said, gesturing to the two chairs in front of his desk as he closed the door behind them. 'Now, can I assume you already know each other?'

'No,' Hugo said. And she looked as mystified as he felt.

'Then I'll introduce you. Dr Walters, this is Hugo Grey, Rosemary's great-nephew. Mr Grey, this is Alice Walters, Rosemary's business associate.'

Since when had his great-aunt had business arrangements? As far as Hugo knew, she'd been living on the income from family investments, most of which ended with her death. 'What business associate?'

The solicitor neatly sidestepped the question by saying, 'My condolences on your loss. Now, Mr Grey—before we begin, we need to follow procedure. I believe you have Miss Grey's death certificate?'

'Yes.' Hugo handed over the brown manila envelope.

'Thank you.' The solicitor extracted the document and read through it swiftly. Clearly satisfied that all was in order, he said, 'We're here today to read the last will and testament of Miss Rosemary Grey.'

Hugo didn't understand why this woman was here. Her name wasn't on the list of people who'd been left bequests. Hugo had assumed that today's appointment was mainly to start the ball rolling with his duties as Rosemary's executor, so he could sort out the funeral.

Philip Hemingford handed them both a document. 'I witnessed the will myself, three months ago,' he said.

The will Hugo knew about dated from five years ago, when his great-aunt had first asked him to be her executor. Why had she changed it—and why hadn't she told anyone in the family?

'Dr Walters, Miss Grey has left you the house.'

What? Rosemary had left her house to a *stranger*?

Wondering if he'd misheard, Hugo scanned the document in front of him.

It was clearly printed.

Last will and testament...
...of sound mind...
To Dr Alice Walters, I leave my house...

A house in Notting Hill was worth quite a lot of money, even if it needed work—work that Hugo had tried to persuade his great-aunt to have done so that she'd keep safe and warm, but she'd always brushed his concerns aside. And Hugo had a really nasty feeling about this. He'd been here before, with something valuable belonging to his aunt and a stranger persuading her to hand it over.

'Just to clarify, Mr Hemingford,' Hugo said, giving Alice a steely look. 'My great-aunt left her house to someone that nobody else in my family has ever heard of before, and she changed her will three months ago?'

At least the woman had the grace to blush. As well she should, because he'd just stated the facts and they all very clearly added up to the conclusion that this woman had taken advantage of Rosemary's kindness. It wasn't the first time someone had taken advantage of his great-aunt. The last time had been Chantelle, the potter who'd befriended Rosemary and told her all kinds of sob stories. Rosemary had given Chantelle her William Moorcroft tea service; Chantelle had sold it to a dealer for a very large sum of money and—worse, in Hugo's eyes—stopped visiting Rosemary. Hugo had quietly bought the tea service back with his own money, returned it to his aunt, and kept a closer eye on people who visited his aunt since then.

Except for the mysterious Dr Walters, who'd slid very quietly under his radar.

Unless… Was this the woman his aunt had mentioned visiting, the one she'd said she wanted him to meet? Hugo, fearing this was yet another attempt by his family to get him to move on after Emma's death, had made excuses not to meet the woman. Fortunately this friend had never been available on Mondays or Thursdays, when Hugo visited, so he hadn't had to deal with the awkwardness of explaining to his aunt that he really didn't want to meet any 'suitable' young women.

Now, he wished he hadn't been so selfish. He should've been polite and met her. He should've thought about his aunt and her vulnerability instead of being wrapped up in his own grief and

his determination not to get involved with anyone again.

'Miss Grey changed her will three months ago,'
the solicitor confirmed, 'and she was of sound
mind when she made her will.'

You could still be inveigled into doing something when you were of sound mind, Hugo
thought. And Rosemary liked to make people
happy. What kind of sob story had this woman
spun to make his great-aunt give her the house?

'There are conditions to the bequest,' the solicitor continued. 'Dr Walters, you must undertake to
finish the butterfly project, turn the house into an
education centre—of which she would like you
to assume the position of director, should you
choose—and re-wild the garden.'

The garden re-wilding, Hugo could understand, because he knew how important his great-
aunt's garden had been to her. And maybe the
education centre; he'd always thought that Rosemary would've made a brilliant teacher. But, if
Rosemary had left the house to his father, as her
previous will had instructed, surely she knew
that her family would've made absolutely sure
her wishes were carried out? Why had his great-
aunt left everything to a stranger instead? And
he didn't understand the first condition. 'What
project?'

'I'm editing the journals and co-writing the biography of Viola Ferrers,' Dr Walters said.

It was the first time he'd heard her speak. Her voice was quiet, and there was a bit of an accent that he couldn't quite place, except it was definitely Northern; and there was a lot of a challenge in her grey eyes.

Did she really think he didn't know who Viola Ferrers was?

'My great-great-great-grandmother,' he said crisply.

Her eyes widened, so he knew the barb had gone home. This was *his* family and *his* heritage. What right did this stranger have to muscle in on it?

'Miss Grey also specified that a butterfly house should be built,' the solicitor continued.

Rosemary had talked about that, three years ago; but Hugo had assumed that it was her way of distracting him, giving him something to think about other than the gaping hole Emma's death had left in his life. They'd never taken it further than an idea and a sketch or two.

'And said butterfly house,' the solicitor said, 'must be designed and built by you, Mr Grey.'

Rosemary had left him a loophole, then. As an architect, Hugo knew what happened if there was a breach of building and planning regulations, or a breach of conditions in a contract. 'So the bequest is conditional. What happens if the conditions of my great-aunt's will are breached?' he asked, trying to sound more casual than he felt.

'Then the house must be sold and the money given to a dementia charity,' the solicitor explained.

Meaning that any scheming done by this Dr Walters would fall flat, and something good would happen with the money. Which was fine by Hugo. It wasn't the money he was bothered about, even though he knew the house would raise a lot of money at auction; it was the fact that this woman appeared to have taken advantage of his great-aunt's kindness, and in his view that was very far from being OK. 'I see,' Hugo said. It looked as if this was going to be easy, after all. 'Then I'm afraid I won't be designing or building a butterfly house.'

'But you have to,' Dr Walters said. 'It's what she wanted.'

Or what Rosemary had been *persuaded* that she wanted, which was a very different thing. Hugo shrugged. 'We don't always get what we want.'

'Rosemary wanted the book finished and the house turned into a proper memorial to Viola,' Dr Walters said, folding her arms and narrowing her gaze at him.

Was that meant to intimidate him? He'd already

survived the very worst life could throw at him. He had nothing left to lose, and he wasn't playing her game.

Philip Hemingford looked uncomfortable. 'This is meant to be a simple reading of Miss Grey's will, not a discussion.'

'That's fine by me,' Hugo said. 'I have nothing to add.' He wasn't letting this woman get away with scamming his great-aunt. And it was going to be very easy to defeat her; all he had to do was refuse to build the butterfly house.

'You can't let Rosemary down,' Dr Walters said, glaring at him.

Oh, was she trying to pretend that she cared? 'Perhaps you'd like to explain, Dr Walters, what your business association was with my great-aunt?'

'As I said earlier, I was working with her on Viola's journals,' she said. 'I'm a lepidopterist.'

The only people Hugo knew who were interested in butterflies were his great-aunt and some of her friends who were from the same generation, all of whom had been slightly eccentric and who hadn't cared about whether their clothes matched or even if they'd brushed their hair that morning. This smart, sleek woman didn't look anything like that kind of person. She looked brittle and fake and completely untrustworthy— much like he remembered Chantelle the potter.

'Indeed,' he drawled, putting as much sarcasm into his voice as he could.

'I lecture on lepidoptera at Roxburgh College at the University of London,' she said. 'Your great-aunt contacted my department and asked if I could help with her project. We've been working on it together part-time for the last six months.'

'She never mentioned the project to me,' he said.

She raised an eyebrow. 'Maybe you didn't talk to her enough.'

Playing that game, was she? His eyes narrowed. 'I was working in Scotland for six months from last October, so I admit I phoned rather than visiting—but I've seen her twice a week since I've been back in London.' Not that it was any of her business.

'Maybe she thought you wouldn't approve of her plans, so she didn't discuss them with you.'

If he'd known of Rosemary's plan to leave her house to a stranger, he would definitely have asked questions. Why hadn't his aunt trusted him? Had this woman coerced her?

'I really don't think this is a helpful discussion,' Philip Hemingford said, looking awkward.

For pity's sake. Why were lawyers so mealy-mouthed? If Hemingford wasn't going to stand up for his great-aunt, then Hugo would. 'Oh, I think it is,' Hugo said. 'I'm sure that professionally you'd want to make quite sure that your client hadn't been cozened into making a bequest. There are laws to prevent such things, I'm sure.'

'As you're such an expert in the law, Mr Grey,' Dr Walters said crisply, before the solicitor could reply, 'I'm sure you'll also be aware of the laws of defamation. I had no idea your great-aunt was going to leave me the house and I certainly didn't ask her to do so.'

'As I wasn't privy to the discussions, I wouldn't know,' he pointed out.

'Exactly,' she said. 'You weren't there.'

Hugo stared at her, outraged. Was she trying to claim that he'd neglected Rosemary? The gloves were coming off, now. 'So if the project goes ahead,' he asked, 'what exactly do you get out of it? Let me see.' He ticked them off on his fingers. '*You'll* be the one to bring any of Viola Ferrers's discoveries to light. *Your* name will appear on any papers written. *Your* name will appear on the cover of the journals as the editor, *your* name will be on the cover of the biography, and *your* name will appear as the director of the education centre. You appear to be doing rather well out of my great-aunt, Dr Walters.' The way he saw it, this woman was using Rosemary to further her career—to further it rather a lot.

'I can assure you, Mr Grey, that Rosemary's name will be on the biography and the journals as co-editor,' Dr Walters corrected, 'and I'll give her full credit on any papers. And, if the education centre goes ahead—which I very much hope it does, because it's clearly what she wanted—then *her* name will be prominent because it was her bequest.' She stared at him. 'And it'll be *your* name on record as the designer and builder of the butterfly house.'

'Ah, but it won't,' he said, 'because I'm not building it. Which means the conditions of the will are breached, so the house will have to be sold and the money given to charity.'

Smug, self-satisfied, *odious* man.

And to think that she'd felt sorry for him in the waiting room—that she'd actually considered going over to ask if he was all right. This man wasn't the sweet nephew Rosemary had mentioned to Alice a couple of times—a man who'd been very busy and struggled to see her. Instead, he was just like Barney and his cronies: posh, entitled and living on a different planet from the rest of the population. This was all just some kind of game to him, and he clearly thought he'd won.

Well, he could think again.

The barely veiled accusation that she was a gold-digger had made Alice angry enough to absorb the shock of the bequest and decide that yes, she'd do this and carry out her friend's dream.

Hugo Grey wasn't going to get his own way. At all. He might be able to sell the house, under the terms of Rosemary's will, but he certainly couldn't dictate who bought it.

Alice didn't have the money to buy the property, let alone turn it into Rosemary's vision. But she could apply to the university for a grant to buy the house, and apply to plenty of other places for grants to do the work to convert it into an education centre and build a butterfly house. If she couldn't get enough money through grants, then she'd crowdfund it. *Help save Rosemary's butterflies.*

This man wouldn't know a butterfly if it came flapping past and settled on his arm. Rosemary did, and Alice wasn't going to let her friend down. The solicitor might have referred to her as a 'business associate', but the elderly lady was more than that; Rosemary had become a good friend over the last six months, and she deserved better than this arrogant, self-centred great-nephew slinging his weight around. A man Rosemary had obviously seen through rose-tinted glasses.

'As you wish,' she said.

He looked surprised.

Did he *really* think she was some kind of gold-digger?

She wasn't sure whether anger or pity came uppermost: anger at the insult, or pity for a man who clearly lived in a world full of suspicion and unkindness. It was a confused mixture of both, but anger had the upper hand. Hugo Grey might be gorgeous to look at, with that floppy dark hair and those cobalt-blue eyes, but he was as much of a snake as Barney.

Let him think that the world would go his way. Too late, he'd find out that it didn't. Not in this case.

'Do you have a key to the house?' he asked.

And, damn, her face was obviously very easy to read, because he nodded in satisfaction. 'I thought so. You need to hand it over to Philip Hemingford.'

No way. Not until she'd managed to rescue the last few journals so she could finish her work. 'As Rosemary left the house to me, I think not.'

'The conditions of your bequest have been breached, so technically the house belongs to the dementia charity she named in the will,' he pointed out coolly.

'I'm not the one who breached the conditions.'

'Really, really,' the solicitor interjected, squirming and looking awkward. 'This isn't…'

'What Rosemary wanted. I agree, Mr Hemingford,' Alice finished. 'And I don't have the key with me.' That wasn't actually true, but she was working on moral rights. Rosemary would've approved of the white lie, she was sure.

'Then I suggest,' Hugo Grey said, with that irritating drawl, 'that you bring the key here to Philip Hemingford by ten o'clock tomorrow morning.'

'Provided,' she said, 'that you do the same. Because the house doesn't belong to you, either.'

He looked shocked at that. 'It's my great-aunt's house and I'm her executor. I'm responsible for it.'

And *she* was responsible for the butterfly project. 'I'll hand my key over when you hand yours over,' she said.

'That,' the solicitor said hastily, 'sounds like a good solution for now. Perhaps you could both bring your sets of keys to me—say, tomorrow at ten?'

'I'm in a lecture at ten, but I can make it at twelve if that works for you.'

'Twelve's fine.'

'Thank you for your time, Mr Hemingford,' she said, giving him a brief nod of acknowledgement. Then she gave the younger man a glance of pure disdain. '*Mr* Grey.' And she hoped he interpreted 'Mr' as 'Entitled piece of pond-life', because that was exactly what she meant by the word.

And she walked out, leaving both men open-mouthed.

Normally, Alice didn't take taxis, but she needed to get to Rosemary's house before Hugo Grey did, to make sure she could still access the journals. So she whistled the first black cab that passed her—to her shock, it actually stopped for her—and took a taxi to the house in Notting Hill.

It felt weird, letting herself into the empty house. Right now the only moving things here were herself and the dust motes dancing in the sunlight.

It was weirder still, not seeing her elderly friend pottering around in the garden, or sitting at the kitchen table with her cup of tea and a welcoming smile.

Tears prickled against Alice's eyelids. Rosemary Grey was special. Kind, eccentric and with a lively mind. In a lot of ways, Rosemary reminded Alice of her grandfather, and she was sure they would've enjoyed each other's company—despite the fact that socially they were worlds apart.

'I'm not going to let him win,' she said fiercely. 'You deserve better than that entitled, spoiled buffoon. I'm going to finish our book. And your name is going on the cover before mine. I'm not going to let you down, Rosemary, I promise. And I keep my promises.'

She went into the study and found the last volumes of the journals. No doubt Hugo would figure out very quickly that she'd taken them and demand them back, so today she'd need to photograph every page and make sure she backed up the images in three places for safety's sake. Hugo Grey and his pomposity were absolutely not going to get in the way of Rosemary's plans.

'We're going to win,' she whispered to the empty house, and locked up behind her again.

Hugo had half-expected Alice Walters to be there, stripping out whatever she could, when he got to his great-aunt's house; but it was empty. Nothing but dust-motes and echoes. His great-aunt's vitality had gone from the place.

He let himself into the garden and wandered through it. The shrubs were overgrown and needed cutting back, but he could smell the sweet scent of the roses and the honeyed tones of the buddleia, and for a moment it made him feel as if his great-aunt were walking right beside him.

The butterfly house.

He could see exactly where Rosemary wanted it. They'd talked about it three years ago, when he'd been so broken after Emma's death and desperately needed distracting. Rosemary had suggested using the rickety old wall at the back of the garden for one wall of it; they'd talked about a house of glass, filled with plants that were the perfect habitat for butterflies.

Rosemary had loved glasshouses. So had he. She'd taken him to see stately homes with amazing conservatories and domes when he was small, as well as the glasshouses at Kew and the Chelsea Physic Garden. They'd had a road trip to the Eden Project, too, when he was in his teens. They'd both been fascinated by the biomes—Rosemary for their contents, and himself for the structure. And Rosemary had been the one who'd championed him when he'd decided to become an architect, specialising in glass.

Had he been so cocooned in his grief that he'd not paid enough attention? He hadn't thought that she'd really meant it about the butterfly house; he'd assumed it was her way of distracting him. Particularly when she'd talked about using the wall of Viola's old conservatory; he'd checked it out and it would've needed completely rebuilding before it could be used to support a structure. He'd assumed that she'd realised the idea was impractical. Had he been wrong?

Standing with his hands in his pockets, he stared at the space in front of him. A lawn that had been cut but not cared for, so it was straggly and patchy, with weeds taking over completely in places. Overgrown flower beds with shrubs drooping, their dead flower heads unpruned. Right at that moment, it was a mess. But, with careful planning and a bit of hard work, he could just imagine the garden transformed and showcasing a butterfly house. A modern twist on a Victorian palm house, perhaps, marrying the past and the present. Something that looked like the past but had modern technology underpinning it; something that would last for the future.

Back in the kitchen, he made himself a black coffee in one of Rosemary's butterfly-painted mugs and sat at the kitchen table.

'What did you really want, Rosemary?' he asked the empty air. 'If the butterfly house was your dream, then I'll back it all the way and I'll build it for you. But if it's this woman trying to use your name and tread on you so she can get to the top, then it's no deal.'

How did he find out which one it was? He knew nothing about Dr Alice Walters. Rosemary had mentioned her friend but Hugo hadn't really paid attention. He'd been caught up in work and brooding—because, without Emma's warmth in his life, he'd been going through the motions. Existing, not living. It had been hard enough to get from the beginning of the day to the end.

Something about this just didn't sit right. It felt as if Alice Walters had taken advantage of Rosemary in the same way as Chantelle had, using a shared interest as a way to befriend her and then cheat her.

He flicked into his phone and looked up the website for Roxburgh College.

And there she was, listed in the staff of the biology department.

Dr Alice Walters.

He clicked on the link. Her photograph made her look much softer than she had in the solicitor's office. Her light brown hair had a natural curl rather than being ironed into the sophisticated smoothness he'd seen. She wasn't wearing make-up, either; her natural beauty shone through and her grey eyes were huge and stunning.

He pushed the thought away. This wasn't about being attracted to a woman who might or might not be a gold-digger. This was about making sure the woman hadn't taken advantage of his great-aunt.

According to her biography on the university's website, Alice had taken her first degree in biology at Oxford, and studied for her Masters and her PhD at London. She was a Fellow of the Royal Entomological Society. Her research interests were in biodiversity, conservation ecology and the impact of land use—all of which fitted with what Rosemary had asked her to do. She'd written an impressive list of papers, including some on re-wilding; she'd been a keynote speaker at several conferences; and she was supervising half a dozen doctoral students.

The academic side of it stacked up.

But were the ideas in the will Rosemary's, or had Alice influenced her? Was Alice Walters involved in this project because she'd liked Rosemary and wanted to help her make a difference, or because she wanted to make a name for herself and had no scruples about taking advantage of others to get there? Had she lied when she'd claimed to have no idea that Rosemary intended to leave her the house?

Until Hugo knew the truth, he wasn't budging.

CHAPTER TWO

Two weeks later, Alice slid into a pew at the back of the church. She didn't want any animosity with Rosemary's family, but she did want to pay her respects to her friend at the funeral. It mattered to her. She'd leave quietly after the service, so the Greys wouldn't even know she was here.

There were lots of people in the congregation; she recognised some as Rosemary's neighbours, and a few of them smiled at her or lifted a hand in acknowledgement. And she definitely recognised Hugo Grey; he was sitting in a pew at the very front of the church, comforting an older couple she guessed were his parents.

The service itself was lovely, with the organist playing Chopin's Nocturne in E flat major as the pallbearers brought in the coffin. 'Morning Has Broken' was the first hymn—if Rosemary hadn't suggested it herself, whoever had chosen it had clearly known Rosemary's spirit well.

When it was time for the eulogy, Hugo stood up and went into the pulpit.

For a moment, Alice caught his eye and it felt like an electric shock.

No, absolutely *no*. It was totally inappropriate to feel that tug of attraction towards someone at a funeral, and it was even more inappropriate because she and Hugo were on opposite sides. During the last couple of weeks, he'd continued to refuse to change his position about building the butterfly house, so Rosemary's house was going up for sale. Alice had responded by putting together a business plan for the university, asking them for a grant towards buying the house and building the butterfly house; she'd also set up a crowdfunding page and a campaign to save the house. Finally, she'd applied for outline planning permission for changing the use of the house and building the butterfly house in the garden.

Everything was going at a speed she wasn't entirely comfortable with, but she had no other choice; she needed to be ready in case Hugo decided to put the house up for immediate auction rather than selling it through an estate agency. Without the money—or at least the promise of it—behind her, she couldn't buy the house and she couldn't fulfil Rosemary's dreams.

She looked away, and Hugo began speaking. Unlike the other day, his voice wasn't full of coldness and sneering; it was full of warmth and affection and sadness. And Alice was utterly captivated.

'I feel as if I should be reading Ophelia's speech up here about flowers, suggesting rosemary for remembrance, because we'll always remember Great-Aunt Rosemary. When I was a child, I spent a lot of time in her garden, and she'd tell me all about the butterflies and the birds and the flowers. So I'm choosing to read something by her favourite poet, Thomas Hardy; Rosemary noticed things, and I remember her reading this to me when I was a child and telling me that the first verse was about butterflies.'

This was personal, Alice thought. Heartfelt.

And the way he delivered it was full of love and meaning. His voice was clear and beautifully modulated; although it didn't wobble in the slightest, because he was clearly determined to do well by his great-aunt, she could see the glitter in his eyes to show that tears weren't far away.

'"When the Present has latched its postern behind my tremulous stay, And the May month flaps its glad green leaves like wings, Delicate-filmed as new-spun silk, will the neighbours say, 'He was a man who used to notice such things'?"'

It was the perfect poem to choose. Just as Hugo had suggested, it was full of butterflies, and it reminded her of Rosemary. Rosemary Grey had definitely noticed things—not just the environment, but also people. Alice had found herself able to open up to the older woman.

A woman who used to notice things.

A woman who was kind and passionate and inspirational.

And Alice was really going to miss her.

Hugo could see Alice Walters sitting at the back of the church. Today, she wasn't the polished, sophisticated woman who'd sat in the solicitor's office and argued with him. She was wearing plain black trousers and a silky black top, and her hair had the slight natural curl he'd noticed in her official university photograph.

Was she here to pay her respects to Rosemary, or to keep an eye on her own interests?

Hugo knew about her crowdfunding bid to buy the house, and Alice Walters exasperated him thoroughly; yet, at the same time, there was something about her that intrigued him.

How ironic that the first woman he'd really noticed since his wife's death was on the opposite side to him. And this was his great-aunt's funeral. He needed to finish his eulogy and give Rosemary the send-off she deserved, not start mooning about a woman he didn't really know and whom he strongly suspected of being an ambitious gold-digger.

So he shared his memories, making sure that

every single person in the congregation—except possibly the woman sitting in the last pew—had something to share, too. Rosemary would want to be remembered with love and with smiles, and he was going to make that happen.

Though he had to hold his mother's hand through 'Abide With Me' and clasp his father's shoulder; the verse about death's sting and the grave's victory caused both of them to stop singing, choked by emotion.

He followed his parents behind the coffin as they left the church; again, he couldn't help glancing at Alice. Her face coloured faintly as she caught his gaze, and he was horrified to feel awareness pulse through him again. Not here, not now, and—actually, no, he didn't want this *at all*. He was done with feeling. It had broken him nearly three years ago, and he never wanted to repeat it.

He'd expected her to be gone by the time the committal had finished, but instead she was talking to some of Rosemary's neighbours in the churchyard. From the way they were chatting so easily to her, he was pretty sure they knew her. Liked her, too, because they were smiling rather than giving her suspicious looks, the way half of them had looked at Chantelle.

Had he judged Alice unfairly?

In which case, he'd really let his aunt down.

Then again, if Alice was as ambitious as he suspected, he didn't want her to get away with using Rosemary. He needed to get to the bottom of this.

Guilt had the upper hand at that moment, so he walked over to her and gave her a nod of acknowledgement. 'Dr Walters.'

'Mr Grey,' she replied, her tone equally formal. 'Perhaps you'd like to join us for the wake?'

Her eyes widened. 'Seriously? I didn't think I'd be welcome.'

Today, her manners were as blunt as the hint of her accent. He rather liked that. It suggested that she was straightforward. Or was that a double bluff from an accomplished and ambitious woman?

'I don't want to cause any upset to your family,' she continued. 'Today's about Rosemary and your memories of her, and I don't want to do anything that takes away from that.'

A gold-digger would've said yes to the invitation without hesitating and would've been charming rather than blunt. Maybe he really had misjudged her. Even though she'd set up that crowdfunding site to buy the house.

This wasn't about Rosemary's house. It was about Rosemary. About saying goodbye. And he needed to do the right thing. The kind thing, as Rosemary would've wanted.

'You'll be welcome,' he said. 'It's in the hotel across the road, if you'd like to join us. I'll leave it to you to decide.' He gave her a nod of acknowledgement, then went to join his parents.

Hugo Grey had actually asked her to the wake. Alice couldn't quite get her head round this. They were on opposite sides. He didn't have to be nice to her. Yet today he'd chosen to be kind.

So she followed the straggle of mourners across the road, accepted an offer to sit with Rosemary's neighbours, drank tea from a pretty floral china cup and ate a scone with jam and cream. Rosemary, she thought, would've enjoyed this.

But all the while she was very aware of Hugo Grey.

The way he read poetry.

The sensual curve of his mouth.

And this had to stop. Even if they weren't on opposing sides, she was absolutely hopeless when it came to relationships. After Barney, she hadn't dated for a couple of years, not trusting her judgement in men, but then she'd met Robin, who'd seemed so nice at first—and the opposite of Barney. Down-to-earth. Except Robin had wanted her to change, too; she hadn't been girly enough for him. After Robin, there had been Ed, who hadn't minded how she dressed—but he'd wanted her to be less of a nerdy scientist, so she'd fit in with his artsy crowd. Then there had been Henry, who'd broken up with her because he'd wanted someone whose career would be less stellar than his.

Everyone she'd dated seemed to want to change her. It didn't matter whether they'd met through work, through a friend of a friend, or a dating app that should've screened them so they were the perfect match.

Maybe she was the one at fault, for picking men who couldn't compromise. And every break-up had knocked her confidence a little bit more.

Not that it mattered, because nothing was going to happen between herself and Hugo. He might already be involved with someone else. All she really knew about him was that he was Rosemary's great-nephew and he was an architect. One who'd won a couple of awards, according to the Internet, and was a rising star in the industry; but she hadn't looked up his private life because it was none of her business.

Even as she thought it, he walked over to her, carrying a cup of tea. 'Dr Walters. May I join you?'

Short of being rude, there was only one thing she could say. 'Of course, Mr Grey.'

'Can I get you some more tea, or something to eat?'

'I'm fine, thanks,' Alice said, suddenly feeling gauche and tongue-tied.

And he clearly wasn't going to make it easy for her, with small talk. He simply sat down beside her and waited.

Given that he reminded her so much of Barney and his entitled friends with their over-elaborate code of manners, was he waiting for her to make a mistake? Not hold her cup properly, or use the wrong bit of cutlery, or…

No. She was being unfair to him, especially as he'd been kind earlier. They were strangers, and this was his great-aunt's funeral. She'd try to meet him on common ground. 'Your eulogy was very good.'

He inclined his head. 'Thank you.'

Wasn't it his turn to make a comment, now, to keep the conversation going?

When he didn't, she added, 'I liked the poem.'

'My great-aunt loved poetry,' he said. 'Hardy was her favourite poet, but she loved Keats as well. And Christina Rossetti—whenever I hear leaves rustling in the trees, I think of Rosemary reading me that poem, or when I see the moon in a cloudy sky.'

Hugo Grey liked poetry? Now that she hadn't expected. But she knew the poems he'd mentioned. '"The moon was a ghostly galleon tossed upon cloudy seas."'

He looked surprised. 'You know that one, too?'

She nodded. 'My grandmother loved that one. She read it to me a lot when I was a child.' And she could hear it in her head, in her grandmother's broad Yorkshire accent.

Just for a moment, the crowded room was forgotten: it felt as if it were just the two of them, the poem echoing down the years to them and joining them together.

'"Watch for me by moonlight. I'll come to thee by moonlight,"' he whispered.

And she could imagine Hugo as the highwayman of the poem, with his breeches and his velvet claret coat, lace at his chin and a French tricorn hat on his hair.

Her mouth went dry as she thought of Bess loosening her black hair in the window, and her highwayman lover kissing the dark waves. What would it be like if Hugo kissed her hair, her cheek, the corner of her mouth?

It made her feel hot all over—and ashamed, because this really wasn't the time or place to be thinking like that. Though, given the sharp slash of colour across his cheeks, she had a feeling that he was thinking something very similar indeed.

And she couldn't make a single word leave her mouth. They were all stuck in her throat.

This was terrifying. She hadn't been this aware of anyone since Barney. But she knew her judgement in men was hopeless and she'd given up trying to find Mr Right. Burying herself in her work had been much safer. Looking at butterfly pheromones and ignoring human ones.

Quoting poetry. How stupid Hugo had been to think that was safe: Hardy, Keats, Rossetti and their images of nature.

But of all things he'd chosen to quote 'The Highwayman'. And it wasn't about the moon as a galleon, the road over the purple moors. It was about Bess the landlord's daughter and the highwayman, the woman plaiting her hair and the man kissing it, promising to be back for her. The jealous ostler with his hair like mouldy hay, betraying the highwayman to the redcoats. Bess saving him temporarily with her own death. Love and passion and death.

Alice Walters's eyes were grey, not dark. Her hair was light brown, almost a nondescript colour, rather than the exotic long, black curls of Bess. She didn't have a red ribbon tied through her hair in a love knot.

And yet remembering the line of the poem made Hugo want to bury his face in Alice's hair.

Would she smell of roses, vanilla or honey?

Oh, for pity's sake.

He hadn't so much as noticed another woman in the last three years. He hadn't wanted to. Emma was the love of his life, and after her death he hadn't wanted anyone else.

So what was it about Dr Alice Walters that drew him, made him actually notice her and react to her like this?

Rosemary would no doubt have said this was a good thing. That Hugo would never forget Emma but it was past time that he started thinking about moving on, finding someone to share his life with rather than spending decades and decades alone. He'd half-suspected that was why she'd tried to get him to meet her friend Ally, and it was why he'd made himself unavailable. He didn't want anyone else.

Maybe he did need to move on. But his first choice definitely wouldn't be an ambitious lepidopterist, a woman whose motives he hadn't yet worked out. He didn't even *like* Alice Walters.

Though he had to acknowledge that he was attracted to her. Not to the glossy, brittle woman from the solicitor's office, but to *this* woman, a woman whose lips had parted ever so slightly and he was incredibly aware of the shape of her mouth. It made him want to lay the palm of his hand against her cheek and rub the pad of his thumb against her lower lip.

And he was at his great-aunt's funeral.

This really wasn't the time or place to be thinking about touching someone, kissing them.

Time seemed to have slowed to treacle. It felt as if he were hearing things from underneath an ocean, slow and haunting like a whale song rather than the trill of birds.

Say something.

He needed to say something.

But moving his lips made him think about *her* lips. How soft they might be against his own. Pliant and warm and—

'Hugo? I'm so sorry about your aunt.'

He looked up. Saved by Millie Kennedy, Rosemary's neighbour.

'Thank you, Millie.' He accepted the elderly woman's hug. 'Have you met Dr Walters?'

'Our Ally? Of course I have. Lots of times. She's been working on Rosemary's book.' Millie hugged Alice, too. 'Good to see you again, love. I'm glad you could make it. Our Rosemary deserved the best send-off.'

Millie was nice to everyone, Hugo knew. But she seemed to know Alice quite well, accepting her as one of her own. And surely a gold-digger wouldn't want to get too close to anyone other than her target, in case she was caught out? So maybe Alice wasn't one of the bad guys. Maybe he'd just become a miserable cynic since Emma's death, seeing the worst in the world.

'I really ought to get back to my students,' Alice said. 'But I wanted to pay my respects to Rosemary.' She stood up, and Hugo realised that without her high heels Alice was a good six inches shorter than he was. Petite. *Cute.*

And it set alarm bells ringing in his head. This woman could be very dangerous to his peace of mind.

'Thank you for inviting me to the wake, Mr Grey,' she said politely, and held out her hand to shake his.

It would be churlish not to shake her hand, he thought. But he regretted the impulse when the touch of her fingers against his made him feel as if an electric shock had zapped through him.

'Thank you for coming to Rosemary's funeral,' he said, equally politely. There were other things he wanted to say, but absolutely not in front of Millie. 'I'm sure we'll be in touch.'

Touch. What a stupid word. His libido seized on it and threw up all kinds of images of her touching him, and he could feel the heat rising in his face.

What was it about this woman that made him feel like a gauche teenager?

And what was he going to do about it?

Alice surreptitiously checked her hand when she left the hotel. Shouldn't there be scorch marks on her skin from where Hugo Grey had touched her?

Because it had felt as if lightning had coursed through her when he'd shaken her hand.

This was crazy.

She didn't react to men like this.

Maybe she was going down with some peculiar virus.

She was very glad to get back to the safety of her office and a tutorial with her students. And she was not going to spend her time mooning over Hugo Grey. She had things to do. Students to teach, Viola's journals to finish editing, a crowdfunding campaign to run...

But it was hard to concentrate. She kept drifting off and thinking about him. Which really wasn't her; she never let anything get in the way of her professionalism. Why was she letting Hugo Grey affect her like this?

'Alice Walters, get a grip,' she told herself out loud. 'He was just being polite when he said he'd be in touch. You're probably never going to see him again. He's going to sell the house, you're going to buy it, and that's that.'

Though she revised her views, the following Monday, when she had the letter from the planning officials rejecting outline permission for the butterfly house.

She'd given them solid reasons for the change of use to the building and the construction of the butterfly house. The fact the planning office had turned her down made her think that someone had pulled strings—someone who clearly had contacts within the department.

And she had a pretty fair idea of who that someone had to be.

Hugo Grey.

Anger simmered in her heart all morning, through all her tutorials, to the point where she had to ask her students to repeat their answers. Her afternoon was scheduled for working on a paper, but she decided to catch up with that later. Right now she had something much more important to do: pin Hugo Grey down and make him fix the mess he'd made.

A quick phone call to his office in Docklands established that yes, he was in, but he was in a meeting until one o'clock.

So far, so good; if she left the university now, she'd reach his office at just about the same time that his meeting finished and she could tackle him face to face.

His office was in part of an old wharf that had been converted; the yellow bricks had been cleaned until they sparkled and the arched windows were huge. Inside, the lobby was light and airy, and the reception area for Hugo's architectural practice was gorgeous, filled with plants and overlooking the river.

'Can I help you?' the receptionist asked.

'I'd like to see Hugo Grey,' Alice said.

'I'm afraid he's in a meeting,' the receptionist said. 'Can anyone else help?'

'Thank you, but I'm afraid it needs to be Hugo himself,' Alice said. 'I'm aware that his meeting's scheduled to finish at one. That's why I'm here now.'

The receptionist looked surprised that the scruffy woman in front of her appeared to possess organisational skills. Alice wished she'd worn her favourite T-shirt, the one with the slogan 'Don't judge a butterfly by its chrysalis'.

'If his meeting overruns, I'll wait,' she said.

'He might not be av—'

'Oh, he'll be available to see me,' Alice cut in, very quietly. 'Unless he'd prefer me to stand in the middle of this waiting area and explain to everyone within earshot why Hugo Grey is completely untrustworthy and they might be better off taking their business to a different practice of architects.'

The receptionist looked alarmed. 'Please don't do that. I'll talk to his PA and see when he'll be available. Would you mind waiting in the reception area?'

'Thank you. I'm Dr Alice Walters and it's about the butterfly house. And,' she added, 'it's quite urgent.'

Three minutes after the receptionist had made the phone call, Hugo came downstairs, frowning.

'Dr Walters? Why are you here?'

'I think you know why.' She folded her arms and glared at him.

'I'm afraid I have no idea what you're talking about,' he drawled.

'So you're a liar as well as a snake?' She gave a humourless laugh. 'I'm sure your clients will be interested to hear this.'

He narrowed his eyes at her. 'We're not going to discuss this here. Come up to my office.' He looked over to the receptionist. 'Thank you, Anjula. I'm sorry you've got tangled up in this.'

Guilt prickled its way across Alice's skin. It wasn't the receptionist's fault that Hugo had behaved this way; and Alice hadn't exactly been very nice to her. 'I'm sorry, too,' she said.

She followed Hugo up the stairs to his office, allowed him to usher her inside and close the door, and took the chair he offered her.

He sat down opposite her and folded his arms. 'So what is all this about, Dr Walters?'

'It's about you pulling strings with your mates at the planning office, Mr Grey.'

'I have no idea what you're talking about.'

She took the letter from her bag and slapped it down on his desk. 'Just what you wanted to happen, I believe. I'm sure you'll be delighted to learn that the council turned down the outline planning permission for the butterfly house—if you don't know that already.'

'That has nothing to do with me.'

She scoffed. 'You seriously expect me to believe that?'

'If a new building or a change of use doesn't fall within the local planning authority's development plan, then a project will be rejected,' he informed her. 'It has nothing to do with any objections that people might raise about the building or the change of use.'

Alice shook her head. 'Rosemary would be so disappointed in you. She really wanted the butterfly house built and the house turned into an education centre, and you're doing your very best to block it. And, just so you know, I'm not a gold-digger. I don't care about money—what I care about is butterflies.'

The woman sitting in front of him wasn't the sophisticated, brittle woman he'd met at the solicitor's office, nor even the quiet, slightly shy woman from the funeral, Hugo thought. This woman glowed. Right from the top of her very messy hair down to her well-worn hiking boots.

For the first time since he'd known her, Alice Walters actually looked like a lepidopterist—like one of Rosemary's hippy friends he remembered from his childhood. Mixed with a bit of Roman goddess. A pocket-sized one, with freckles on her snub nose.

She was still speaking. 'Did you know that three-quarters of British butterflies are in decline, and the number of moths has gone down by a third in the last forty years?'

He didn't.

'They're not just silly little flappy things that we don't need to worry our pretty little heads about. Butterflies are important as pollinators—they don't have the fur of a bee for the pollen to stick to, but they cover more ground than bees and that means greater diversity in the gene pool. They're important in the food chain, both as prey and predator, and they're important indicators of the health of the ecosystem. Butterflies and moths are fragile, so they react quickly to change, and if they vanish it's an early indicator of problems in an area.'

This was way outside his area of expertise. But she was clearly both knowledgeable and passionate about her subject, and that passion drew him like a magnet. No way was he going to stop her speaking—even if she did have a few of her facts wrong about the planning application.

'They're important in teaching children about the natural world,' she continued, 'and the transformation during their life-cycle from egg to caterpillar to pupa to butterfly.' She ticked the points off on her fingers. 'And if nothing else they're beautiful. Just look at the delight on a child's face when they see butterflies in the garden or the park or the forest. We need all the beauty we can get in this world.'

He remembered being delighted by the butterflies in Rosemary's garden, as a child. And, now he thought about it, there didn't seem to be as many of them around as there had been when he was young.

But this woman was also accusing him of something he hadn't done, and that wasn't acceptable. 'So you think it's OK to march into my office and be rude to my team, without having a shred of evidence of what you're accusing me of?'

'In the solicitor's office, you said you refused to build the butterfly house, meaning that the conditions of the will aren't met and Rosemary's house will have to be sold,' she said. 'And you're an award-winning architect, so it's obvious that any planner will take notice of what you have to say. If you put in an objection, it'll carry more weight than a normal person's.'

'That isn't how planning works,' he said. 'Did you take advice before you submitted the outline application?'

She folded her arms. 'I might have an accent, but that doesn't mean I'm stupid.'

Interesting. She was chippy about her background? Then again, she'd been to Oxford. Having the wrong accent might've made things harder for her there.

'So you took advice.' He tried to make it sound like a statement rather than a question.

'Yes.'

'May I?' He gestured to the envelope she'd slapped down on his desk.

'Help yourself.'

The angry colour on her cheeks was subsiding, now. But she was still slightly pink and flustered, and Hugo had to stop himself wondering what she'd look like if she'd just been kissed. Would she be equally pink and flustered? Would her eyes glow with that same passion?

He forced himself to concentrate on reading the letter. Then he looked at her. 'Judging by their objections, whoever you went to for advice on your application obviously didn't explain what you wanted clearly enough. Did you submit plans? Sketches? Anything to scale?'

'It was an *outline* planning application. I was told it didn't need anything like that.'

'Sketches and plans would have helped. And a proper explanation.' He looked at her. 'You could talk to someone at the planning department and ask them if modifying your application would change their decision.'

She narrowed her eyes at him. 'Are you offering to help me, now?'

'I...' He raked a hand through his hair. Yes and no. He *could* help her; he just wasn't sure if he wanted to. 'My great-aunt was lovely. She was kind, she was generous, and people took advantage of her.'

Her mouth opened in seeming outrage. 'I wasn't taking advantage of Rosemary. I'd never do that. Apart from the fact that I'm not the gold-digger you seem to think I am, she was my *friend*.'

'Philip Hemingford introduced you to me as her business associate.'

'I was her friend, too. I liked her. She was straightforward. She judged people on who they were.'

That chimed with him. But Alice also flustered him—and she made him angry when she added, 'Rosemary mentioned her high-powered nephew. But you never seemed to be around.'

'I had a six-month project in the wilds of Scotland. It's not exactly easy to pop in to Notting Hill from several hundred miles away.'

'What about after your project ended?'

'I visited twice a week—obviously on days you weren't there. But you're welcome to check with her neighbours, if you want proof. Mondays and Thursdays, to be precise.' He stared at her, challenging her to call his bluff. He'd enjoy seeing her back down and apologise, confronted with the proof.

She met his gaze head on, to make the point that he didn't intimidate her.

It felt as if there should be a military drummer in the room, rat-tat-tatting a challenge.

Just when the tension reached screaming point, she inclined her head. 'Your eulogy convinced me that you loved her.'

The quiet words took all the combat out of it. She was acknowledging that, even though she knew nothing about him, she could tell he'd loved his great-aunt.

Maybe it was his turn to make a concession. 'And her neighbours knew you. Millie liked you; she didn't have any time for Chantelle.'

She frowned. 'Who was Chantelle?'

'Someone who befriended Rosemary a few years ago, told her massive sob stories, and as a potter she fell in love with Rosemary's William Moorcroft tea service—so my great-aunt gave it to her.'

'What's William Moorcroft?' Alice looked mystified.

'It's Art Deco china. Pretty—and also worth a great deal of money.' He took his phone from his pocket, did a quick search and then showed her a photograph.

She bit her lip. 'Oh, no. I broke the handle off

one of those cups, a couple of months ago. I glued
it back on, but…' Her eyes widened as she obviously noticed the auction price guide. 'Oh, my
God. I thought it was just a pretty cup and it was
one of Rosemary's favourites, so I mended it. I
had no idea it was worth that sort of money. It
should've been done by a proper specialist. I'm
so sorry.' She blew out a breath. 'I'll pay for a
proper repair.'

And right at that moment Hugo knew that Alice
Walters was absolutely genuine and he'd misjudged her. This wasn't a woman who'd tried to
inveigle his aunt into leaving the house to her so
she could make lots of money. This was a woman
who shared Rosemary's love of butterflies and
wanted to help her reach her dream. A woman
who'd mended a cup she'd thought was worth
only a couple of pounds rather than throwing it
away, because it was his great-aunt's favourite;
and now she knew it was valuable she was offering to pay for a specialist repair.

'Don't worry about it,' he said. 'But Chantelle
wasn't the only one who took advantage of my
great-aunt over the years, simply the last of them.
There were a few others.'

'I'm sorry. That's a horrible thing to do. Betraying someone's trust is just vile.'

There was something heartfelt about her words,
and he wondered who'd betrayed her.

'I had absolutely no idea about her will,' Alice said. 'When I got the solicitor's letter, I thought maybe she might have left me some of Viola's specimens for the university collection. I didn't know she'd planned this. And, even though I love the idea of setting up a proper education centre and a butterfly house in Rosemary's name, I do understand that you wouldn't want all her estate going to a stranger.'

'Technically, it goes to charity,' he pointed out.

'Whatever.' She spread her hands. 'What *does* matter, though, are Viola's journals.'

'The ones you took from the house,' he said. He'd discovered that when he'd looked in the office.

'I returned them to the solicitor, the next day, along with my key. And he gave me a receipt for them, if you'd like to see it.' She paused. 'You obviously know that Rosemary was having trouble with her hip.'

No, he hadn't. His great-aunt was of the generation that just got on with things and didn't make a fuss. She hadn't mentioned a word about a problem with her hip.

'That's why she gave me a key—so she wouldn't have to get up and limp to the front door to let me in every time I visited.'

And now he felt bad. Why hadn't he known? Why hadn't he *noticed* that Rosemary actually let him do things for her instead of being her usual fiercely independent self? He'd been so busy trying to keep himself looking like a functioning human being that he'd had tunnel vision, and it made him feel ashamed. Had the trouble with Rosemary's hip had anything to do with her having a stroke?

'I loved working on the journals with her,' Alice continued softly. 'You've no idea how amazing it is, seeing words that are nearly a couple of centuries old, and hardly anyone else has seen since they were written. Sketches and watercolours that are still as fresh as the day they were painted. And, best of all, to hear about the person who created those journals from someone who actually knew her when she was still alive.'

'Actually, I do,' he said.

She blinked. 'You've seen the journals?'

'When I was younger. I just liked the pictures of butterflies. I was too little at the time to try and work out what the handwriting said. But when I was a student I saw the original plans for the Kew Gardens palm houses and it made all the hairs stand up on my arms—so I'm guessing that's how you felt about the journals.'

'It is,' she confirmed. 'Viola Ferrers deserves her place in lepidopterist history. And Rosemary, too. She was a custodian. She kept Viola's work safe, and the butterfly collection intact. Something that I think is worth sharing with the nation, the way Rosemary wanted it—starting with having Viola's study restored to how it was, because it's important for social history as well as scientific history.'

This wasn't a gold-digger talking. At all.

Hugo saw this with clarity, now. Alice didn't want the house for herself. She wanted it for the butterflies. She wanted it to make a *difference*.

'I have a site meeting this afternoon,' he said, 'and I think this is a discussion that needs a bit longer than a lunch break.'

Hope bloomed on her face. 'Are you saying you're going to work with me instead of against me?'

He wasn't promising anything. Not until he'd looked at everything properly. 'I'm saying,' he said, 'that we should talk further. Are you available this evening?'

'Yes.'

He liked the fact that she hadn't tried to make him feel as if she was doing him a favour, claiming she'd have to shuffle things round to accommodate him. Clearly this project was important to her, and as far as she was concerned anything else could be moved. That was a good sign.

'We should meet on neutral territory,' he said.

'The obvious place,' she said, 'would be Rosemary's house. Except neither of us has a key any more.'

Because he'd backed them both into a corner at the solicitor's office, and he knew it. 'OK. I'll get one of the keys back. For today,' he said. 'Until we've talked. What time can you meet me there?'

'Any time. I'm working on a paper this afternoon, so I can be flexible.'

'Five-thirty, then?' he suggested.

'That works for me.'

He held out his hand to shake hers.

Big mistake.

Just like the last time he'd shaken her hand, every nerve-end in his skin felt electrified.

Given that she suddenly looked pink and flustered, did it affect her the same way? Though he couldn't allow himself to think about that. This was about his great-aunt and the butterflies. Nothing else.

'I'll see you out,' he said, and ushered her down to the reception area.

And why was it that he found himself watching her walk away? Why was it that he was starting to feel things he'd thought were damped down for ever?

This was a potential complication that neither of them needed. By the time he met her at his great-aunt's house, he'd better have his head and his emotions completely back under control.

CHAPTER THREE

As Hugo had agreed to meet her at Rosemary's house, Alice hoped there might be a chance he was going to listen to her and have a proper discussion about the butterfly house instead of being the bull-headed, irritating man who'd judged her without examining the evidence properly. Which in turn meant that he might actually help her to fulfil her promise to Rosemary. If he agreed, then the money she'd raised so far in crowdfunding could be used for renovations, repairs and building the butterfly house, rather than the whole lot having to be used to buy the house itself.

Hugo Grey was a businessman first, so she needed to show him the plans she'd made for grant applications. Plans that showed potential footfall and revenue, so he could see that the project would be self-supporting. And then she'd show him the things that really made a difference: Viola's journals, her butterfly collection and the garden itself. She knew he'd probably seen them all before—but she was also willing to bet that he'd never seen them from her particular point of view.

Armed with her laptop, Alice took the Tube to Notting Hill and walked to Rosemary's house. Hugo was already there waiting for her, leaning against the gate. She'd expected him to let himself inside to stake his claim to the house; the fact that instead he'd waited for her outside made her feel a lot more relaxed about the situation. Though, at the same time, her heart skipped a beat as she drew nearer to him. His cobalt-blue eyes really were stunning. He'd changed into jeans instead of the sharp business suit he'd worn in the office and taken off his tie; it was odd how such tiny differences could make him look so much more approachable.

'Thanks for meeting me here,' she said.

'You're welcome.'

Was she? Was that mere politeness, or did he actually mean it? She'd never been able to tell with Barney's set. She'd taken them at face value—and then she'd learned that they'd been laughing at her all along, mocking the working-class girl who'd been stupid enough to think that the privileged classes would ever accept her for who she was.

'Shall we?' He gestured to the front door; once he'd unlocked it, he stood aside for her to enter.

She caught her breath as she walked into the

kitchen. 'It doesn't feel right, being here without Rosemary.'

'That's how I feel, too,' he admitted.

'I'd always put the kettle on and make us some tea before we started work on the journals.'

'Proper loose-leaf tea, and make sure you warm the pot first,' he added.

She could almost hear Rosemary saying that; clearly it had been the same for him when he'd visited. She looked at the teapot on the dresser. 'Given what I know now about the tea service, I don't think I'd dare use that teapot ever again. I'd be too scared of dropping it. I can't believe she let me think it was just ordinary.'

'I can,' he said wryly. 'She once told me not to save things for best. She said you need to use things *now* and enjoy them, rather than save them for a special occasion that might never come.'

'She was full of wise words.' Alice felt her voice thicken in her throat. 'I miss her.' But getting emotional wasn't going to help anything. She needed to keep this businesslike. Professional. She looked at him. 'But that's not why we're here.' She set her laptop on the kitchen table. 'What do you want to start with, the journals or the butterfly house?'

'The journals,' he said. 'I assume you had copies made when you borrowed them.'

'Yes. I photographed them myself.' She looked

him straight in the eye. 'And, before you ask, the reason I took them was in case you refused me access. I promised Rosemary I'd finish writing Viola's biography and editing her journals, and I think it's important to keep promises.' Especially as she knew how it felt when someone broke a promise to you. 'Just so I don't waste time running through stuff you already know, what do you know about Viola Ferrers?'

'She was born in 1858 into a fairly wealthy family, and she followed the fashion of Victorian women collecting butterflies,' he said promptly. 'Her husband bought this house when they married, and it's stayed in the family since then.'

'OK. First off, Viola was a proper entomologist, so please don't dismiss her as an amateur collector with a "little hobby",' Alice said, making quote marks with her fingers and giving him a hard stare. 'She was much more than that. She studied butterflies scientifically. She wrote papers, though because she was a woman she never got to hear her papers read at the Linnean Society—just like Beatrix Potter.'

He blinked. 'That was a reason for them not to read her papers? Because she was a woman?'

'Oh, they *read* the papers, all right,' Alice said. 'But Viola wasn't allowed to hear them being read. At the time, women weren't allowed to be members of the society. She couldn't even go along to meetings as a guest. But she didn't let any of that nonsense stop her studying butterflies. Let me show you.'

Again, Hugo noticed how vital and animated Alice was when she talked about the project; he really, really liked that. He followed her into Rosemary's study, and she took one of the narrow leather-bound books from the shelf.

'I know you've already seen them, but I want to put them in an academic context for you. Viola kept these journals from the age of sixteen,' she said. 'She used them as a sketchbook as well. She travelled around the country to see botanical gardens; she wrote down the details of the butterflies she saw there and sketched them, too.' She opened the book, flicked through a couple of pages and held the book out to him. 'See?'

Viola's handwriting was very neat and regular, and Hugo noticed that all the diagrams were labelled. 'She's called the butterflies by their Latin names,' he said, surprised; that hadn't registered when he'd been young. There was a water colour of a copper and black butterfly on the page Alice showed him. *'Boloria euphrosyne.'*

'The Pearl-bordered Fritillary. It used to be widespread throughout the country, and now it's mainly found in parts of Scotland, Cumbria, Devon and Cornwall,' Alice said, looking sad.

'They're one of the early spring butterflies; their caterpillars feed on violets.'

'I'm not sure I remember ever seeing any of these in real life,' he said thoughtfully.

'There are some specimens in Viola's collection.' Alice went over to the large display cabinet, opened one of the drawers and slid out one of the frames. 'Here.'

It was a long, long time since Hugo had seen the frames of butterflies. And it still amazed him that these specimens were more than a hundred and fifty years old, yet the colours were still fresh. 'That's beautiful. And also really sad, because—well, shouldn't butterflies be flying, not pinned to a board?'

'I'm glad you said that,' Alice said. 'I agree. Though at the same time we do need to curate the collectors' frames we still have. So many of these haven't been kept properly and the butterflies have just crumbled into dust over the years.'

'I remember Rosemary showing me the big blue butterflies when I was very young,' he said. 'They fascinated me.'

'Those would've been tropical ones from South America,' she said. 'I'm guessing that was *Morpho didius*. That's one of my favourites, too.' She put the frame back carefully and fished out another. 'Here.'

'That's what I remember,' he agreed. 'The colour. Though obviously I've never seen a live one.'

'You wouldn't, in England, unless you've been to a butterfly house. Though there are some blue British butterflies,' she said. She tipped her head very slightly to one side, as if thinking about something, and then said, 'I could show you.'

'In London?'

She nodded. 'Or a bit further afield.'

She was asking him to go on a butterfly expedition with her?

Right then, she looked exactly like what she was: a butterfly specialist. Scruffy, not caring about fashion in the slightest, and totally in love with her subject.

'All right,' he said. Because going further afield with her wasn't the same as going on a date, was it? Alice was proposing a scientific expedition to back up her argument on the butterfly house project, and as he was on the opposite side it made sense for him to accompany her so they were both in full possession of all the facts.

But what if it was a date?

He checked himself. Of course it wasn't. Though, if he was honest with himself, Alice Walters intrigued him. And he was definitely attracted to the scientist, the woman who glowed with passion when she spoke about her subject.

That snub nose. The freckles. The light in her grey eyes.

Reining in his thoughts, he brought the subject back to the butterflies. 'The specimens in these frames: are they butterflies that Viola collected herself?'

Alice nodded. 'She went on expeditions abroad. In Victorian times, you didn't actually need a passport to travel, so we don't have exact dates of when she went. But she wrote up her expeditions in her journal. Some of her specimens are in the British Museum.'

Hugo hadn't known that, either. 'And that's important?'

'It means the specimens are of really, really high quality. Lots of collectors in those times offered specimens to the British Museum and were rejected.'

'And hers were accepted? That's pretty special,' Hugo said.

'Exactly. You should be proud of her,' Alice said. 'And she didn't get the specimens solely from expeditions; she used to breed butterflies here in this garden, working out what food plants and habitats helped to produce the best specimens.'

Now he was beginning to understand why Alice thought the journal project was so important. 'And that was rare for a woman in her time?'

'Probably not,' Alice said. 'A lot of women did academic work that their husbands took the credit for—which isn't me having a feminist rant at you, it's just stating how things were back then. Women couldn't even study at university until a decade after Viola was born. Even when they were allowed to attend university, at first they couldn't graduate; they were given a certificate of completion for their exams rather than a proper degree.'

'I had no idea,' he said.

'The University of London was the first one to allow women students and the first one to confer degrees on women. Viola studied there—at my college, which is why Rosemary contacted me in the first place—and she fell in love with one of her fellow students. Luckily for her, he was pretty enlightened and he encouraged her to keep up her scientific work, even after they got married. She bred her butterflies, did her experiments and wrote papers for entomology magazines.' Alice folded her arms and gave him a level stare. 'And I think her name should be a lot better known.'

'Did my great-aunt do something similar?' he asked. What Rosemary actually did had always been a bit of a mystery to him.

'Yes. But she took photographs of butterflies, rather than going out with a net and a killing jar. That's how I do things, too. I want to conserve butterflies, not preserve them.' Alice put the frame back in the cabinet. 'Which leads me to the butterfly house. Shall we go into the garden?'

'Sure.' He went to the back door; after he'd unlocked it, he stood aside so she could lead him into the garden.

He noticed there were several butterflies resting on the buddleia, soaking up the sunshine.

'Peacocks,' she said, seeing his gaze. 'The blue eye-spots make it obvious why they get their common name—but I bet you didn't know they hiss.'

He stared at her. 'Really? Butterflies *hiss*?'

'Well—it's not *actual* hissing,' she amended. 'It's their third line of defence against predators. The first one is the underside of their wings looking like a leaf; if a bird works out that it's potential food and not a leaf, then the butterfly will open its wings to flash those eye-spots—it's called a startle display. If that doesn't make the bird back off, then the butterfly rubs its wings together and it sounds like hissing.'

'That's amazing.' Hugo could see now why Rosemary had wanted Alice to set up the educational centre. This was the sort of fact that would hold a child spellbound. The way Alice talked held *him* spellbound, too.

'Butterflies are amazing,' she said. 'That buddleia needs a bit of work so it'll have better growth next year. But you already know from Rosemary's will that she wanted the garden properly re-wilded and filled with plants that attract butterflies and bees.'

'And a winding path through it, so you don't see the butterfly house itself until the very last minute.'

She stared at him. 'That wasn't stated in her will, but it's something she said to me a couple of times. So did she discuss it with you?'

'Years ago, but…' He didn't want to tell Alice why he'd needed distracting. He didn't want her to start pitying him. 'There was a lot going on in my life at the time. I guess I didn't pay enough attention to what she was telling me. She hadn't said anything to me about it for quite a while, so I thought she'd shelved the idea.'

'And now?'

'I don't know.' He looked at her. 'You're not like you were at the solicitor's.'

'Not wearing a suit and make-up and high heels, you mean?' She rolled her eyes. 'I'm a scientist, not a fashion plate.'

'So that's what you normally wear for work?' He gestured to her faded jeans and ancient khaki T-shirt.

'Yes.' She shrugged. 'If you're doing field-work, wearing strappy sandals is the quickest way to give yourself a sprained ankle, wearing a dress with bare legs instead of trousers tucked into boots will make you vulnerable to ticks, and little strappy tops are no protection at all against sunburn. So I dress sensibly.'

'I don't think I've ever met anyone who wears hiking boots,' he said.

She frowned. 'Surely you have to wear boots and a hard hat on building sites?'

'If it's a working site, like the one I went to this afternoon, yes. Otherwise, ordinary shoes will do.'

She looked at his feet and raised an eyebrow. 'Handmade Italian shoes are *ordinary*?'

Why did that make him feel so defensive? 'They're comfortable.'

'They're the male equivalent of Louboutins.'

Although her tone was slightly acidic, there was a little glint of amusement in her eye. She was teasing him—and, now he thought about it, he was enjoying being teased.

He hadn't felt like this in a long, long time. It was the sort of comment Emma would've made to him.

Emma.

Loneliness washed over him. Would he ever stop missing his wife? Would he ever stop wishing he could turn back time and turn down the invitation to that conference, so he would've been there when Emma had that fatal asthma attack and he could've saved her?

He didn't want to dwell on his feelings, so he switched the topic back to something safe. 'So how do you see the butterfly house working?'

'Rosemary had photographs of the orangery that used to be here—the one Viola used when she bred her caterpillars. There might even still be traces of it on the wall.'

'And you think it should be recreated?' he asked.

'No, because we'll be using the building for a different purpose. We'll need a mix of butterflies, and that includes tropical ones,' she said. 'And I need the kind of tech that means we get the right intensity of light and humidity, as well as the right temperature; the plants can't do all the work. And we need a good design.' She paused. 'Which is where you come in.'

Two choices: he could design the butterfly house, or he could block everything.

He thought about it again. A butterfly house. A confection of glass. A house of dreams.

He loved working with glass, and he was so tempted to build it. 'What sort of thing are you thinking about? A biome, like the ones at the Eden Project?'

'It could be anything you like. The butterfly house at London Zoo is shaped like a caterpillar, and the one in Vienna is a gorgeous Art Nouveau building. The way I see it, you're the glass and architecture specialist. Your imagination is the limit. Well, and the site itself,' she amended. 'Obviously the shape of the garden and the way the sunlight falls will affect what you build.'

He liked the fact that she'd realised that.

A glass building. Complete freedom with the design. Fulfilling his great-aunt's dream. This was the perfect commission. 'The Palm House at Kew,' he said. 'That was the first glass building I fell in love with. And glass domes. Like the one at the Reichstag in Berlin with its double staircase.'

'A dome filled with butterflies free to fly wherever they like. Kind of like a snow globe, except summery,' she said thoughtfully.

Alice Walters actually got it, Hugo thought. She understood the kind of stuff that filled his head. Knowing that made his skin prickle with excitement.

'There isn't really room to build a dome in the garden here. And I'm not making any promises,' he said, 'but maybe we could look at the possibilities.'

'That would be good.' She smiled at him—the first genuine smile she'd ever given him—and it made him catch his breath. It felt as if the world had just flashed into technicolour for a moment before fading back to its usual monochrome.

For pity's sake. He had to get a grip. This wasn't about him. Or her. It was about his great-aunt's dreams and whether they could make it work.

Her stomach rumbled audibly, and she winced. 'Sorry. I kind of forgot about lunch today.'

She'd turned up at his office at lunchtime, he remembered, and thrown that hissy fit on him. 'Because you were too angry with me to eat?'

'Something like that,' she admitted, wrinkling her nose. 'And then I was busy.'

He forced himself not to think about how cute she looked. 'We could get a pizza delivered.' Just to make sure she didn't think he was coming on to her, he added, 'Seeing as we still have a lot to discuss about Rosemary's project, we might as well refuel while we work.'

'Pizza's fine by me,' she said. 'We'll go halves.'

He liked that, too. She hadn't assumed that he was going to pay, just because it had been his suggestion.

Sharing.

Could they share? Was this their chance to start compromising? 'There could be a topping issue,' he said. 'Pineapple or no pineapple?'

'I don't object hugely to pineapple,' she said. Then she tipped her head on one side. 'But olives are essential.'

It sounded as if she was thinking the same thing: they needed to find common ground so they could start negotiating properly. Negotiation by pizza... He'd started it, and she seemed to be running with it. He might as well see where it took them. 'OK. Ham?'

She gave a deep, dramatic sigh. 'Oh, *please*. Prosciutto cotto at the very least.'

He couldn't help grinning. 'You're a pizza snob—and you were lying about the pineapple, weren't you?'

'Yes. I was trying to be conciliatory. I'm prepared to agree to your demands for pineapple,' she said. 'But if you want deep pan or stuffed crust, the deal's off. Proper pizza comes in thin crust only.'

He wasn't quite sure whether she was teasing him or whether she was serious. She was a bit more difficult to read than he'd expected. 'Did you ever eat pizza with Rosemary?'

'Generally I use fresh basil on pizza,' she said, her expression deadpan and her voice dry.

That was a definite tease. Nobody in his life teased him any more.

And then it hit him.

Obviously Alice didn't know about Emma, because she wasn't treading on eggshells round him the way everyone else in his life did; she was reacting to him as if he was a normal human being.

And he really, really liked that feeling. It was refreshing enough for him to want to spend more time in her company. 'All right. Thin crust, olives, pineapple, prosciutto cotto. Anything else?'

'No. That all works for me.'

'It's a deal.' Once he'd called the local pizzeria and arranged delivery, they headed back to the kitchen. 'So how would the education centre work?' he asked.

'We might need to remodel the inside of the house. For a start, we need an exhibition room,' she said. 'And a space where children can learn how to help butterflies and wildlife by doing practical things—planning their own butterfly gardens with food plants for both caterpillars and for butterflies, how to build a bug hotel, that sort of thing. I'd like a screen where they can see things like a time-lapse film of a butterfly going through its life stages.' She tapped into her laptop. 'Like this. It's only a couple of minutes long, but it always wows my first-years and I think you might enjoy it.'

He watched the film in silence, marvelling at the photographer's skills. 'That's amazing. I had no idea it was that complicated.'

'And that's only on my laptop. Imagine seeing that on a really big screen, then following the trail through the garden, seeing those exact plants growing, seeing butterfly eggs on leaves and caterpillars munching their way through plants, seeing pupa suspended from canes or even hatching, and then seeing butterflies flying round in the butterfly house. How cool is that?'

Very. But he needed to be businesslike about it. This couldn't be a decision based on emotions. 'Rosemary's investment income died with her. There isn't any money to fund the running costs of an education centre.'

'Which is why we need grants,' she said. 'We can do some crowdfunding, to cover the set-up costs, and then the grants will help keep us going. We'll also charge admission fees—reasonable prices, though, because we want schools to visit in term time and families to visit out of term time. And we also want to attract anyone who's vaguely interested in butterflies or conservation or re-wilding, or just wants a nice morning out with friends. So we'd have a pop-up café on the patio, serving drinks and healthy food. Probably a shop, for books and postcards and butterfly-related goods. I've put together a business plan with some projected footfalls, for my grant applications.' She opened another file and let him look at it. 'I can email this across to you, to give you time for a proper read.'

'That would be helpful,' he said, and gave her his business card with all his contact details so she could send the file across to him.

'Do you think you could pause the house going on the market, just until you've seen what the possibilities are and had time to make an informed decision?' she asked.

She wasn't asking him to stop the sale completely, he noticed. She was giving him the choice of continuing their discussions, but without making assumptions that he'd fall in with her plans.

'And what I've put together so far isn't set in stone,' she said. 'It's simply a start. A working document for discussion, if you like.'

'So my family could have input.'

She inclined her head. 'Including the butterfly house design, which Rosemary wanted to be yours. Though maybe I should take you to visit a few, so you can see what sort of things are possible.'

He remembered what she'd said earlier about site visits to see blue butterflies. 'So you're suggesting we should visit butterfly houses and botanical gardens.'

'Butterfly houses,' she said, 'and sites of scientific interest. I suppose we could include formal botanical gardens, but as we're looking at re-wilding the garden I think it would make more sense to look at nature reserves, so you can see the kind of habitat we can try to create.'

This was treading a very fine line indeed between a date and a business proposition.

He wasn't sure if the fluttering in his stomach was terror or excitement. Probably both.

'I appreciate,' she said, 'that you have demands on your time from work—as do I. But maybe we can look at our diaries and find a few windows for field trips: some local, some a bit further afield.'

Now Hugo could see that Alice Walters wasn't the ambitious gold-digger he'd first thought she was, he was more inclined to listen to her.

'All right,' he said. 'I'll tell Philip Hemingford to put the sale of the house on hold for a couple of weeks and we'll do some field trips.'

'Thank you.'

He looked at her. 'What about your crowdfunding?'

'That stays,' she said. 'If you decide to put the house on the market after all, the trust will need all the money we can get. If you don't sell the house, then the money will pay for remodelling and building the butterfly house.'

'Trust?' He narrowed his eyes at her. 'What trust?'

'I was thinking, it should be called the Ferrers-Grey Butterfly Education Trust,' she said. 'Honouring both Viola and Rosemary. Oh, and that reminds me: we should have a garden centre section of the shop with butterfly-friendly plants and seeds, obviously including violas and rosemary.'

Acknowledging his great-great-great-grandmother and his great-aunt with plants as well as with the name of the building? He liked that. But that still left him with questions. 'What about you?'

She frowned. 'What do you mean?'

'Don't you want your name on the project?'

'I told you before,' she said quietly, 'it isn't about me. It's about the butterflies. And I'm disappointed that you still think I'm doing this because I'm some power-crazed, ambitious bitch. Clearly you mix with the wrong sort of women.'

He felt the flush of embarrassment and awkwardness creep under his skin. 'I'm sorry. I didn't mean it quite like that.'

'No?' Her eyes narrowed a fraction.

The pizza arrived, at that moment; when he came back from answering the door, he gave her a wry smile. 'Can we agree to a truce over dinner?'

'I guess. How much do I owe you?'

'This one's on me,' he said, cutting the pizza into slices. 'Next meeting, you buy the pizza or whatever.'

Without further comment, Alice fetched plates from the cupboard and cutlery from the drawer and found two glasses. 'Water?'

'Thank you.'

It was weird, sharing a pizza with a near-stranger, one who'd been pretty much hostile up until now.

And Alice found herself feeling unexpectedly shy with him.

Oh, for pity's sake. Just because he was posh, it didn't mean that he was superior—or even that he had a superiority complex. She really had to stop letting what had happened with Barney get in the way of how she handled things. She was older, wiser and much more able to hold her own.

And she needed to be practical about this. 'I could do a field trip on Saturday,' she said. 'Would that fit in with you, or do you need to check with your partner?'

For a second, it was as if someone had closed a shutter over his expression. And his voice was very cool when he said, 'No partner.'

Uh-oh. Did he think she was coming on to him? Maybe she ought to invent a boyfriend. Then again, her love life was a complete disaster zone. Better, perhaps, to suggest something else. 'If you want anyone else from your family to come along, that's fine. Where I have in mind can be rough ground, though, and it's also prime tick season, so I'd recommend whoever joins us wears strong shoes and trousers that can be tucked into socks.'

'That's fine,' he said. 'It'll be just me.' He looked at her. 'Is your partner going to be OK with it?'

'I,' she said, 'am married to my butterflies.' Just so it would be clear to him that she saw this purely as work.

Her fingers accidentally brushed his as they reached for a slice of pizza at the same time, and again she felt that weird flicker of electricity along her skin.

Even if she admitted to being attracted to Hugo Grey, she wasn't going to act on it. Her relationships never worked out, and she wouldn't let anything jeopardise the butterfly project. 'OK,' she said, cross with herself when her voice went slightly breathless. She made an effort to sound professional. 'Do you mind an early start? It'll take us about three hours to get to the first site, maybe more if we get stuck in traffic.'

'How early?' he asked.

'Given that the butterflies I have in mind are usually more active in the morning, six o'clock?'

He looked wary; maybe he wasn't a morning person. 'OK. I'll pick you up.'

'I'll pick *you* up,' she corrected. 'Let me know your address.'

For a moment, she thought he was going to argue, but then he nodded and gave her his address. 'Do you need anything from Rosemary's study, while we're here?' he asked when they'd finished eating.

'No. I've already got copies of the photographs she had of Viola.'

'OK. I'll clear up here, then, and I'll see you on Saturday.'

'All right. I'll email over the files I promised you.' She paused. 'Thank you. I appreciate you listening to what I had to say.'

He inclined his head. 'And I apologise for my earlier prejudice.'

She appreciated that apology; and it was her turn to compromise, now. 'I can understand it, now you've told me about the people who took advantage of her. In your shoes, I think I would've felt the same. Maybe we both started off on the wrong foot.'

'Maybe,' he agreed.

'Can I help with the washing up?' she asked, glancing at the crockery on the table.

'No, it's fine. See you Saturday.'

'Saturday, six a.m. sharp,' she echoed, closed her laptop and left the house.

This field trip absolutely wasn't a date: it was part of a business proposition. So why were all her senses humming?

Probably, she thought, because Hugo Grey was the first man who'd attracted her like this in several years.

But nothing was going to happen between them. She needed to be sensible about this. Her

She wore absolutely no make-up, and her light brown hair was tied back with a brightly coloured silk scarf, though little tendrils had already escaped at the front. Next to the women he was used to at the office in their sharp business suits, she should've looked a scruffy mess: but actually she looked incredibly cute, completely natural and guileless. When she smiled at him, his pulse actually leapt.

Oh, help.

He didn't want to be attracted to anyone. Particularly to someone whose life had almost nothing in common with his.

He needed to get a grip.

He also needed more sleep.

Why on earth had he agreed to this ridiculous field trip at this even more ridiculous time of day?

'Good morning. Ready to go?' she asked.

How could she possibly be this chirpy at six o'clock? 'You're a morning person, then,' he muttered.

Her smile broadened. 'Of course. It's the best part of the day. You've already missed the sunrise.' She raised an eyebrow. 'Owl, are we?' And then, just to make it worse, she gave a soft, mocking 'Tu-whit, tu-whoo.'

He glared at her, his synapses not firing quite quickly enough to let him make a suitably sarcastic retort.

relationships always ended in disaster; and she and Hugo were pretty much complete opposites. Well-worn hiking boots versus handmade, highly polished Italian shoes. It simply wouldn't work, so it was pointless letting anything start.

Even if he did have the most gorgeous eyes…

CHAPTER FOUR

DURING THE REST of the week, Hugo found himself thinking about the butterfly project whenever he had a spare moment. The doodles on his desk blotter were all of potential butterfly house designs—except for the sketches that started to creep in on Friday morning. Little line-drawings of a woman with untamed hair, a snub nose and freckles.

Sketches of Alice Walters.

Not good.

He didn't want to start thinking about Alice, or about anyone else. Emma's death had broken him; although on the surface it looked as if he'd managed to put himself back together, deep down he wasn't so sure he had. Without her, there was a huge hollow in the middle of his life and he didn't know how to fill it. His family and friends had encouraged him to date again, saying he needed someone in his life to stop him being lonely. But Emma wasn't replaceable. And anyway he didn't want to risk loving and losing again. It was easier just to avoid social situations and use work as an excuse. The only person he really saw much of nowadays was his best friend, and—since an incident where Kit and his wife had tried to set him up with a suitable woman, and Hugo had backed off for a couple of weeks—Hugo's non-existent love life was a topic firmly off limits.

Saturday's butterfly expedition with Alice was a field trip, not a date. Hadn't she told him herself that she wasn't interested? You didn't tell someone that you were married to your job if you were even vaguely interested in dating them. This was business.

He dragged himself out of bed on Saturday morning at what he considered an unearthly hour, showered and dressed, ate a banana for breakfast, and was considering whether he had enough time to make himself a coffee to wake himself up properly when his doorbell rang.

Six o'clock precisely.

At least Alice was punctual. He would've been seriously annoyed if he'd dragged himself out of bed and then she'd made him wait around for ages.

She was wearing bright red canvas shoes instead of hiking boots today, he noticed when he opened the door to her. Her faded jeans emphasised her curves, and the slogan on her equally faded T-shirt was very pointed: 'Don't judge a butterfly by its chrysalis.'

She just laughed. 'You can always nap in the car, because it's going to take us about three hours to get there, if we're lucky with traffic. Or, if you need coffee, I've a flask and a spare reusable cup in my backpack.'

Of *course* she'd have reusable cups. 'Thanks.' Though he was aware of how ungracious and grumpy he sounded, and winced inwardly.

She glanced at his feet. 'I'm glad you're not wearing your posh shoes. I forgot to warn you that it can be a bit boggy underfoot in the wetlands.'

'Wetlands? I thought we were looking at butterflies?'

'We are. But one of the sites we're visiting is in the Norfolk Broads.' She spread her hands. 'By definition, it can be a bit wet.'

'Oh.' He looked at her feet again. 'No hiking boots for you, today?'

'They're in the car. I don't drive in them,' she said.

'I'm a bit surprised someone with your green credentials has a car,' he said.

She smiled. 'I don't. But if I can't get somewhere any other way, I hire one.'

'Oh.' And then he felt stupid.

'Feel free to change the temperature or the music,' she said when he'd climbed into the passenger seat.

She was being nice, and he was being impolite

and grouchy. 'This is fine,' he said. 'And sorry. I don't mean to sound grumpy.'

She patted his forearm, and his skin tingled where her fingertips touched him. 'Poor little owl. I promise what we're going to see will be worth the early start. Well, as long as the weather holds.'

'Butterflies don't like rain?'

'Or wind. They like calm, bright weather,' she said. 'Or just calm will do. Overcast is all right, if there isn't a wind. I have something with me in case I need to cheat a bit, though.'

'Cheat?' He was mystified.

'Later.' She started the car. 'Go back to sleep, if you want to.'

Hugo had no intention of doing that, though he was glad that she didn't want to chatter inanely. However, lulled by the warmth of the sunlight through the windows and the soft piano music she was playing in the car, he did actually doze off; when he opened his eyes again, they were in the middle of nowhere. The road before them wasn't even a proper road; it appeared to be a dirt track.

'Where are we?' he asked.

'Milk Parsley Fen—named after one of the plants that grows here.' She drove through a gap in the hedge into what seemed to be a field, though there were a couple of other cars parked underneath the trees. 'Do you want some coffee before we go for a walk?'

He wasn't going to cut off his nose to spite his face. 'Yes, please.'

'It's black, no sugar,' she warned. 'I never quite got out of my student habits.'

'That's fine. Coffee's coffee,' he said.

She took a backpack from the back seat, removed a metal flask and two cups, and poured them both a coffee.

'Thanks. Butterflies on your cups?' he asked as she fitted a silicone lid to a cup and handed it to him.

'Of course.' She changed into her hiking boots, put the backpack on her shoulder and slung a camera round her neck. 'Ready?'

'Ready.' The coffee was already making him feel more human. He followed her down a narrow path; the ground felt a bit spongy to walk on, and there were fronded grasses everywhere he looked. But what he'd expected to see was absent.

'There aren't any butterflies,' he said, knowing he sounded accusatory and a bit like a spoiled child denied a promised treat, but not being able to stop himself.

'They're probably skulking around in the reeds,' she said. 'Wait until we get further in. The reserve managers have cut some paths through the fen so we'll get a decent view of the milk parsley, but at the same time the really vulnerable plants aren't in danger of being trampled on.'

He could follow that line of thinking. 'So paths need to be cut in a re-wilded garden?'

'Absolutely. These are wetlands, so they're not quite what Rosemary had in mind—but there's a specific butterfly I want you to see here,' she said.

There was a stream running alongside them, he noticed, and a small bridge; as they drew closer, a large swan waddled out of the reeds and sat in the middle of the bridge, staring at them.

'Looks as if we're going to have to wait for a bit,' she said.

'We can't just walk past the swan?'

She shook her head. 'My guess is his mate and his cygnets are somewhere nearby. He's likely to be a bit protective. Let's give him some space,' she said. 'Look—there's a Painted Lady and a Peacock.' She gestured to the purple flowers lining the route, and he could see butterflies resting on the plant with their wings outstretched.

And then, all of a sudden, he could hear a kind of peeping noise.

'Cue the cygnets,' she said with a smile.

The swan stood up and started to walk over the bridge, his movements slow and deliberate.

'Let's follow him,' she suggested.

The peeping noise grew stronger; the swan veered off to the side, shaking his tail as he stepped towards a large pool. And then he glided majestically across the water towards another swan and a bevy of cygnets, whose peeping noises grew even louder.

'I love this.' Alice took Hugo's free hand and squeezed it. 'You can just hear them yelling, "Hurry up, Dad, we're going exploring!", can't you?'

He would never have thought of that if he'd been on his own; but now she'd said it he could almost hear it. 'Yes. And I don't think I've ever seen anything like this before.' And now she was holding his hand it felt as if she was leading him into an enchanted landscape. Part of him was skittish—he hadn't expected to hold hands with anyone again—but part of him felt as if he was being drawn back to life. Step by step. Noticing tiny details he'd blanked out before.

He stared at the swans and their cygnets, entranced as they glided to the other side of the pool and then filed out of the water again, the adults walking at each end of the line with the cygnets protected between them. 'That's *such* a privilege.'

'Isn't it just?' Then her eyes widened as she clearly realised that she was still holding his hand. 'Sorry. I tend to get a bit carried away when I see things like this.'

'It's fine.' But how crazy was it that he actually missed her holding his hand when she took her fingers away from his?

They carried on through the marshes, with

Alice pointing out various butterflies. It was a long time since Hugo had seen that many butterflies in a single place, and it amazed him. The birds were singing; the sun was bright and warm; and, even though there had been other cars in the field where she'd parked, they hadn't seen another human since they'd arrived. It felt a bit as if they were wandering through some kind of magical oasis.

'I think I'm going to have to cheat a tiny bit,' she said, 'because there's one particular butterfly I really, really want you to see. We're right at the start of first brood, and the weather's almost perfect, but I'm not taking any chances. I don't want you to miss this.' She took the backpack from her shoulder and removed a bunch of sweet williams, which she placed carefully on the ground.

He looked at her, surprised. 'Are butterflies super-attracted to these flowers, then?'

'Yup,' she said, coming over to stand next to him. 'The caterpillars only eat milk parsley—which is why the fenland in this part of the country is the main habitat for them—but the butterflies just love them. It's a combination of the scent and the nectar.' She smiled. 'And now, we wait. I probably should've warned you that there's a bit of waiting around on field trips.'

Hugo, who absolutely loathed wasting time, was a little surprised to discover that he didn't actually mind waiting around with Alice. Time didn't seem to be important when he was with her. It felt as if he was in a different place, somewhere much more carefree than his usual regimented life.

And then he saw it flying gracefully over the reeds before it landed on the bunch of flowers: a butterfly the size of his palm, creamy yellow and black, with a dark blue line and two red spots on the lower pair of wings, which curved down like a swallow's tail.

'That's incredible,' he whispered.

'An English Swallowtail,' she whispered back. '*Papilio machaon.* You only find them here in England in the Norfolk Broads.'

She'd brought him here to see a rare butterfly. The biggest butterfly he'd ever seen flying. And all of a sudden he got why she loved the creatures so much. He was spellbound by it.

Spellbound by her.

Not that he was going to let himself think too much about that. He didn't feel ready for this.

She'd taken the camera out of its case and was taking photographs of the butterfly; Hugo's attention was caught between them both, the concentration and the joy on Alice's face and the sheer beauty of the butterfly.

Once the butterfly had taken its fill of the nectar from the sweet williams, it flew off again.

'That,' he said, 'was stunning. I know you said you only find them around here, but is it possible to get them to breed in London?'

'Not native ones. They'd have to be imported,' she said, 'and they'd need to live in a butterfly house.'

She didn't say anything more. Hugo realised she was letting the butterflies make the case for her.

'And look there,' she said.

He followed where she was pointing, to the gorgeous turquoise insects darting about. 'Dragonflies?'

'Damselflies,' she said with a smile. 'If we're lucky, we'll get to see some rare dragonflies as well.'

He was entranced by the whole thing. She was right: it was definitely worth the early start. And, best of all, on the way back to the car they saw some more Swallowtails flying across the fen and landing on a patch of yellow flag irises.

'That,' he said, 'was amazing.'

'I'm glad you enjoyed it. The first time you see a Swallowtail is a bit special.' She smiled at him. 'And now we're going north. Not wetlands, this time—I want you to see the kind of wildflower meadow that I think would work with Rosemary's plans.'

'Bring it on,' he said.

* * *

That smile gave Alice hope that the butterflies were convincing Hugo to give the project a chance.

Yet, at the same time, his smile worried her because it made her heart feel as if it had done a backflip. Nearly all the men she'd fallen for in the past had hurt her—letting her think they wanted her for who she was, yet then they'd wanted to change her. She wasn't posh enough, wasn't girly enough, was too nerdy...

What you looked like shouldn't matter. But, in Hugo's world, it did. And Hugo himself was a fashion plate, with his designer shoes and sharp suits; it was so obvious that she'd be setting herself up for yet another crack in her heart, if she let herself fall for him. She didn't want to take that risk. It would be much more sensible to keep things strictly business between them and avoid the heartache in the first place. As for the way he made her stomach feel as if it swooped, the way her skin prickled with awareness whenever he accidentally brushed against her—she'd just have to ignore it.

It was an hour's drive to their next site and she kept the conversation light on the way. As she drove into the nearest village, Hugo's stomach rumbled audibly.

'Is that a hint you want to stop for lunch?' she asked.

He winced. 'Sorry. We had an early start. I only had time for a banana for breakfast.'

'If you'd said,' she told him, 'we could've stopped on the way for a bacon sandwich.'

'Your butterflies distracted me.'

'They'll do that,' she agreed with a smile. 'Look, there's a pub just up here. Let's stop and grab some lunch.'

She insisted on paying for their paninis and coffee, on the grounds that he'd bought the pizza earlier in the week, then drove them out of the village.

'So this is somewhere else in the middle of nowhere?' he asked wryly.

'That's why it's called a field trip.' Though then Alice made the mistake of looking at him, and the expression in his eyes caused her pulse to jolt again. Worse still, she noticed the curve of his mouth. How easy it would be to reach out and run a fingertip along his lower lip…

She pulled herself together with an effort, parked the car on the verge of a narrow country road, then led him down a track between two high hedges.

'It's as if that little brown butterfly's leading us,' he said.

'It's a Ringlet—*Aphantopus hyperantus*,' she said.

'Named after the little circles on its wings?'

She smiled. 'Absolutely.'

At the end of the track, they reached a stile with an information board next to it.

'This place is an Iron Age fort?' he asked, sounding surprised.

'It's the best-preserved Iron Age fort in East Anglia,' she said, 'and it's home to a lot of butterflies. This place always blows my students' minds, so I hoped you'd like it.'

'Are we actually allowed to walk among this?'

'We are indeed.' She indicated the people walking along the top of the massive circular earthwork; others were halfway down the steep slopes with cameras, bending down and clearly taking photographs of butterflies. 'Come and take a look.'

They made their way to the top of the outer circle. 'The wind's got up a bit, so the butterflies will be looking for sheltered spots,' she said. 'We might see more on the slopes than we do up here.'

'So all the flowers on the slopes and down in the middle of the rings are wildflowers?' he asked.

'And grasses,' she said. 'There are some rare orchids here, but you'll find the common flowers here as well—red clover, oxeye daisies, that sort of thing. And this is pretty much how I'd see Rosemary's re-wilded garden looking.'

'All different colours,' he said, 'like a kind of

kaleidoscope. I can see that working.' He frowned. 'What's the shimmery stuff?'

'Butterflies,' she said. 'Stand still for a moment and watch.' Though she found herself looking at Hugo rather than at the butterflies; she enjoyed seeing the expression on his face change as he realised that there were lots of butterflies on the wing, just above ground level. She loved the way he'd clearly just realised how magical their surroundings were, the way his eyes lit up with pleasure as he worked out exactly what he was seeing.

'Blue butterflies,' he said. 'Just what you promised me.'

'Not quite as spectacular as the Morphos in Viola's collection,' she said, 'but I adore the Chalk Hill Blues. The females are actually more brown than blue, but they both have all these pretty circles on their underwings.'

'To make them look more like leaves if a bird happens to be passing?' he asked.

So he'd actually been paying attention to what she'd told him, and remembered it? Funny how that made her feel warm inside. 'Yes.'

To stop herself doing anything stupid—like holding his hand again—she took her camera out of its case and snapped a few pictures of the butterflies. They wandered round the hill fort, walking on the slopes as well as the top, and every so often Hugo stopped to watch the butterflies, looking entranced.

'I can't remember the last time I saw a blue butterfly,' he said. 'Or quite as many butterflies in one place. They're beautiful. Thank you for bringing me here.'

'My pleasure,' she said, meaning it. 'I can take you to some reserves nearer London, next time. I just wanted to show you these two places today.'

'I'm glad you did. It's been a while since...' He stopped.

She said nothing, giving him the space to talk, and eventually he said, 'Since I've been anywhere that made me feel this light of heart.'

The butterflies, the landscape—or sharing it with her? Though she didn't quite dare ask him, because she didn't want him to turn back into the grouchy, suspicious man she'd first met.

'So what made you choose to study butter-flies?' he asked.

'My grandad used to take me to the park on a Sunday afternoon and show me all the butterflies on the plants there, whether they were the culti-vated lavender in the posh bit or the wildflowers by the hedges,' she said. 'He died when I was ten. I was torn between studying botany and lep'
tery, but I think he would've been pleased
my career choice.' She glanced at him
about you? Why architecture?'

'I guess, like a lot of kids, I liked building things with toy bricks. I spent hours and hours creating things. And then I noticed the way things were built, whenever I went out. I loved the Natural History Museum—but it wasn't just because of the dinosaurs or the big blue whale. I liked the shape of the building and the windows, and the colours of the bricks.' He smiled. 'Rosemary took me to Kew when I was about ten, and I fell in love with the Palm House. It's all the light. That's why I like working with glass.'

Alice really didn't understand what made Hugo Grey tick. But maybe this was her chance to get to know him better. 'What's your favourite thing you've designed?' she asked.

'The project I've been working on in Scotland for the last year,' he said. 'It's a country house on the buildings at risk register.'

'So you like restoring old buildings rather than designing new ones?'

'A mixture of the two,' he said. 'But this one was a bit special. There's a glass dome in the centre of the main hall—sadly, there were only a few fragments of the original glass left, but at least we had some photographs to work with. And there's an amazing spiral staircase beneath the dome.'

The tone of his voice made Alice feel sure that o felt the same way about staircases and glass domes as she did about butterflies. So maybe they weren't quite as far apart as she'd thought.

'So that's what you specialise in? Domes and staircases?'

'Glass and staircases,' he said. 'Some historic, some modern.'

He was surprisingly easy to talk to, now she'd got him onto his favourite subject. She really enjoyed the drive home, to the point where she didn't want the day to end. When she finally parked in his road, it shocked her that she actually felt a lurch of sheer disappointment that their trip was over.

Maybe he felt the same, because he said, 'Would you like to come in for a coffee?'

She did—and, at the same time, she didn't. Getting close to him made her feel twitchy. She opened her mouth to make a polite excuse, and was surprised to find herself saying, 'That'd be nice.'

From the outside, his house was a Victorian redbrick terrace, with large windows and a front door with a very fancy arch of glass above it. Inside, the house was startlingly modern and minimalist, with the walls painted a soft dove-grey and the flooring pale wood. The hallway had a flight of stairs leading off it; and a door to the left led to an enormous living room with an old-fashioned fireplace, a sofa and a desk with a drawing table. Though there was no artwork of any description on the walls, she noticed, just a very workmanlike clock. No bookshelves, either; or maybe all his shelves were hidden in a clever architectural way.

He shepherded her into a kitchen with white marble worktops, dark grey wooden cupboards and rectangular white tiles on the walls; the lighting was very modern, almost industrial. At the far end of the room there was a dining table and chairs; but what caught her eye was the entire wall of glass looking out onto the garden.

'That's spectacular,' she said. 'Was it like this when you bought it?'

'No. I opened it up,' he said. 'The glass doors fold inwards, so in summer you can open up the whole wall and step straight from the house to the garden.'

She loved the idea of it; though the garden was as minimal as the house, with a stone patio containing a bistro table and a couple of chairs, a square lawn mown very short indeed, and that was it. No shrubs. No herbaceous border. Not even a pot containing a plant of some kind. There wasn't a flower in sight.

'It's lovely,' she said, meaning that it *could* be lovely if he put a bit of effort in. Though maybe, as an architect, he saw the building rather than its surroundings. Given how minimalist the house was, the garden matched it. Though in her view that garden was all wrong. If it were hers, she'd fill it with roses. There would be herbs and shrubs to attract butterflies and bees. And there would most definitely be a wild patch at the end, with cornflowers and poppies and clover and vetch. Maybe a tiny pond. It would be glorious.

'Espresso?' he asked, breaking into her thoughts.

'Thanks. That'd be nice,' she said politely.

'Feel free to grab a seat.' He indicated the dining table by the glass wall.

And of course he had a posh coffee machine—a proper bean-to-cup machine that ground the beans and made coffee with the perfect *crema* on top, which he brought over to her in a double-walled glass cup.

Posh.

So very different from her world.

Hugo belonged in Barney's world—and she never had. Even though she knew Hugo was trying to make her welcome, she couldn't help remembering the way Barney's set had reacted to her, scoffing that the girl from the council estate really thought she could step into a world of privilege.

You don't belong here, the voice said in her head.

But Hugo had asked her here without a hidden

agenda. Feeling wary was ridiculous and stupid, and she needed to stop it. Right now.

To shut the voice up, she asked, 'So do you have any photographs of the house you were working on?'

'Yes.' He took his laptop from a drawer, tapped a few keys, then slid it across the table to her. 'All the photographs are in the same album. Help yourself.'

'Thanks.' She scrolled through them. 'Wow. I can see why you fell in love with it. That's an incredible staircase. And that glass dome...'

'It's pretty special,' he said. 'It's as near a reproduction to the original as I could get. And we managed to save all the original glass that was left in the external windows.'

'That's impressive,' she said, handing the laptop back to him.

Again, when her fingers brushed against his, it made Hugo's skin tingle.

What was it about this woman that drew him?

He was seriously tempted to ask her to stay for dinner, but he knew it would probably be wise to put a little distance between them, so he could get his head back in the right place.

So he kept the conversation light until she'd finished her coffee. 'Thank you for today,' he said. 'The butterflies were amazing.' And then his mouth ran away with him and spoiled his good intentions. 'Are you busy tomorrow?'

'Do you want to do another field trip?' she asked.

'I was thinking we could take a look at some glass,' he said. 'The British Museum, perhaps, and then Kew.'

'All right,' she said. 'I'll meet you at the British Museum. It opens at ten—is that too early for you?'

'It's a lot later than today,' he said wryly, 'so it's fine.'

'Ten o'clock on the steps,' she said.

He nearly—nearly—kissed her cheek, but managed to hold himself back.

And he intended to spend the rest of the evening working with figures and formulae, until he'd got himself back under his usual control. He was absolutely not going to kiss Alice Walters.

'See you tomorrow,' he said, shepherding her out to the door.

And when he closed the door behind her, he realised that he was regretting not kissing her.

Utterly ridiculous. He'd get a grip before tomorrow. For both their sakes.

CHAPTER FIVE

HUGO FELT LIKE a teenager about to go on his first date with a new girlfriend. Given that he was meeting a lepidopterist, how ironic it was that he had butterflies in his stomach.

Today was supposed to be about his great-aunt's legacy. But his heart still felt as if it had done a somersault when he walked through Bloomsbury and peered through the railings around the British Museum to see Alice standing on the steps beneath the famous pediment, waiting for him. As she'd done the previous day, she was wearing faded skinny jeans; when he drew nearer, he saw that today's T-shirt bore the slogan 'Butterflies do it with pheromones'.

'Nice T-shirt,' he said.

She grinned. 'Here's your fun fact for the day: a male butterfly can sense female butterfly pheromones from ten miles away.'

'Ten miles?' Was she teasing him?

His confusion must've shown on his face, because she smiled. 'Really. I'm full of facts like that.'

'They must have amazing noses.'

'Butterflies don't actually have noses, the way we do,' she said. 'They smell with their antennae and taste with their feet. If you'd said you wanted an anatomy lesson, Mr Grey, I would've brought one of my presentations with me.'

Anatomy lesson. Why did that suddenly make him feel hot all over? For pity's sake. The last woman Hugo had dated was his late wife. He'd closed down his emotions and his libido since Emma's death—at least, he'd thought he had. But, since he'd met Alice, that part of him seemed to have woken up again. She'd shown him things on their field trip that had enchanted him, and now the woman herself was enchanting him. Everything from that sassy slogan on her T-shirt, to the sparkle in her grey eyes and the way she smiled when she'd spotted something that interested her.

'I don't need an anatomy lesson, Dr Walters,' he said—a little more brusquely than he'd intended, because she really flustered him. 'Besides, today is about glass.'

'Indeed. Time to strut your stuff, Mr Glass Expert.'

But there was no mockery in her eyes. She actually looked interested.

Interested in glass, or—his heart skipped another beat—interested in him? He wasn't sure whether the idea scared him or thrilled him more.

Keep it professional, he reminded himself, and ushered her into the Great Court. 'This,' he said, 'is one of my favourite buildings in London.' That was it. Talk about his passion for architecture. Don't think about emotions. Keep it focused on the abstract. Something *safe*. 'I love the way the shadows of the steel beams change as you walk round.'

Hugo's gorgeous blue eyes were suddenly all lit up as he talked about the roof, and he'd lost that slight grouchiness. Clearly he felt the same way about glass as she did about butterflies, Alice thought. And seeing him in love with his subject made him so much easier to deal with.

Though, at the same time, it made him dangerous. Mesmerising.

She needed to get a grip; she'd been burned too often by men she'd been attracted to and then it had all gone wrong. That wasn't going to happen again. 'Tell me about the glass,' she said.

'There are three thousand, two hundred and twelve panes in that roof,' he said. 'And no two are identical.'

'Seriously?' She couldn't understand how you'd build a roof from what seemed to be a jigsaw puzzle. Besides, to her most of the panes looked identical.

'Seriously. It's because the roof undulates,' he

The nectar guides.' She gestured to one of the
nts in the lawn. 'To a butterfly, this yellow
delion looks white at the edges, but red at the
tre where the nectar is. And a horse-chestnut
ver is yellow to them when it's producing nec-
and red when it's not.'

That's amazing,' he said, smiling. And that
e made her heart feel as if it had done a back-
He actually listened to what she said. So far,
adn't tried to change her.

ould she take a risk?

r should she be sensible, and find a way of
ng some distance between them?

t she couldn't. As they walked through the
ens together, their hands brushed against
other. Once. Twice. And then their fingers
ocked, just one at first, and then another, and
er, until they were actually holding hands.
e could barely breathe.

is wasn't supposed to be happening.

ey were absolutely *not* a couple.

here they were, holding hands, as if they
on a proper date. It was thrilling and terri-
all at the same time.

is is what I wanted to show you. The Palm
,' he said. 'Victorian glass and iron.'

s it her imagination, or did his voice sound
unny? As if he was just as flustered by this
happening between them as she was, and

said. He took his phone from his pocket, flicked
into the Internet and brought up a photograph.
'This is it from above.'

It was nothing like she'd expected. 'It looks like
a turquoise cushion, with an ancient brooch in the
centre—but, from down here, the glass seems
clear. And what's that in the centre?'

'It's the dome of the old Reading Room,' he
said. 'And, actually, it's not very much smaller
than the dome of the Pantheon in Rome.'

She stared at him, as amazed by the statistic
as he'd seemed when she'd explained about butterfly pheromones. 'Seriously? But it looks tiny!
I've been to Rome, with my best friend, and the
Pantheon's enormous.'

'Which shows you just how huge this courtyard
is—it's the biggest covered square in Europe,' he
said. 'I would've loved to work on something like
this, merging the old and the new.'

Just as he had with the Scottish country house
and its dome, she thought. Could he be tempted
to build something new—the butterfly house—
that would fit into the garden of Rosemary's old
house?

Together, they walked around the Great Court;
just as Hugo had said, the light and the pattern of
shadows changed as they moved round the area.

'This is pretty stunning,' she said. 'Though I'm

not sure we could make a design like this work for a butterfly house.'

'It wouldn't.' He smiled. 'You wanted to show me an amazing butterfly yesterday, before you showed me the wildflower site. I wanted to show you my favourite bit of new architectural glass before we go and see the other stuff.'

'It's spectacular,' she said. 'Obviously I've been here before, but I never really noticed it. You've shown it to me in a very different way.'

'Like your Iron Age hill fort yesterday,' he said. 'I know this is going to make me sound a complete heathen, given the treasures within these walls, but I'd really like to skip the rest of the building now and go to the second bit of our field trip.'

Field trip. Of course that was what it was. They were going to Kew together because of the butterfly house project, not because he wanted to spend time with her, she reminded herself. Part of her wanted it to be a date; but at the same time part of her was scared she'd be sucked into trusting someone again and end up being let down. Pushing away the mingled disappointment and wariness, she said brightly, 'Sure.'

At Kew, they grabbed a quick coffee and a sandwich, then wandered through some of the formal gardens; Alice laid her palm against Hugo's upper arm to direct his attention to some

butterflies, and instantly regretted the when her fingertips started tingling w touched him.

'Butterfly,' she said, knowing how sounded. For pity's sake, she should be to him in full sentences, not mumbl words at him. What was wrong with was she being so inarticulate?

'What is it?'

Focus on the science, she told he your hand off his arm. Stop being *Focus.* 'It's a *Polygonia c-album—* monly known as a Comma.'

'Because of the shape of its wing asked.

She liked the fact he'd tried to be because of the white mark on its ur

'I love the colour. Especially the the purple flowers.'

'It's not necessarily purple to a said.

His eyes widened. 'It's not?'

'They don't see colour and res way that humans do—even though in the back of their head and near and-sixty-degree vision, they ca detail,' she explained. 'And they traviolet patterns on flower peta

'What ultraviolet patterns?' h

he was trying really hard to keep it businesslike…
and failing, the same way she was.

'It's like an upside-down ship,' she said.

'Well spotted. It was the first glasshouse built
on this scale,' he said, 'so they used techniques
from shipbuilding. And here you see sixteen thousand panes of glass.'

He let her hand go when he opened the door
for her—but within moments they were back to
holding hands. Neither of them said a word about
it or even looked at their hands to draw attention
to what was happening. But it was there. A fact.
They liked each other enough to hold hands. And
Alice wondered if Hugo, too, was feeling the little
fizzy bubbles of pleasure that seemed to be filling her own veins.

The fact that Hugo really seemed to be considering building the butterfly house made her heart
feel light with hope.

She had no idea how long they spent wandering through Kew, exploring the glasshouses and
the gardens, with Hugo pointing out his favourite bits of various buildings and herself pointing out the butterflies flitting over the plants. All
she could really concentrate on was the warmth
of his fingers curled round hers, and how good
it made her feel.

Time blurred, seeming to go in the blink of an
eye and yet stretch for a week at the same time.

But finally the gardens were closing and all the tourists appeared to be heading for the exits.

'Time to leave, I guess,' Hugo said, sounding regretful.

'I guess,' she said.

They walked back to the Tube station together. Alice knew they'd be taking completely different trains—Hugo to Battersea and herself to Shadwell. He'd sounded wistful earlier; would he want to prolong the time with her and maybe suggest dinner? Should she suggest it, maybe? Or were they back in the real world again, now they'd left the glasshouse behind? Would he want to put some distance between them?

'Thank you for a nice day,' Hugo said, which pretty much sealed it for her.

Distance it was.

Separate trains and separate lives.

She could ask him if he'd like to have dinner with her; but perhaps it would be better to spare them both the embarrassment of him refusing. Instead, she smiled. 'I enjoyed it, too. Thank you for showing me the glass.'

He looked awkward, as if debating something in his head; and then he bent forward and kissed her swiftly on the cheek.

Warmth spread through her, along with some courage. 'Maybe we can go to see a butterfly house, next.' She took a deep breath. 'Wednesday afternoons are usually free for me.'

He took his phone from his pocket and checked something. 'I can do Wednesday, this week.'

They were talking as if this was a business appointment, but it felt like a date. And she was shocked to realise how much she wanted it to be a date.

Forcing herself to sound calm, she said, 'We could meet at Canary Wharf station at, say, one o'clock?'

'I'll put it in my diary,' he said. 'See you then.'

'See you then.' She held her breath, just in case he decided to lean forward and kiss her other cheek—or, even, her mouth.

But he didn't.

He just smiled at her and walked away.

Was she about to make a colossal fool of herself? Should she back off?

But all the same Alice found herself touching her cheek when she sat down on the train, remembering how his lips had felt against her skin.

Would he kiss her again, the next time they met?

Would it be a proper kiss?

And, if so, what was she going to do about it?

Butterfly fact of the day: a butterfly's body temperature needs to be thirty degrees C before it can fly.

Alice regretted the impulse, the second she'd sent the email.

Supposing Hugo thought she was trying to flirt with him?

Well, she *was* trying to flirt with him. Even though her head knew it was dangerous and reckless and a very bad idea, that flare of attraction was strong enough to make her ignore her common sense. She couldn't stop thinking about the way he'd held her hand all afternoon, and that kiss on the cheek, and wondering just how his mouth would feel against hers.

He didn't reply. Which served her right, and she forced herself to concentrate on her students and stop mooning over him. But, at the end of the day, there was an email waiting in her inbox.

Glass fact of the day: when glass breaks, the cracks move at three thousand miles an hour.

Flirting by nerdiness?

It was delicious. And addictive. She sent him a nerdy fact by text on Tuesday morning; he replied in kind, later in the day. By Wednesday lunchtime, Alice was practically effervescent with excitement. She couldn't wait to see him.

Just as they'd arranged, Hugo was waiting for her at Canary Wharf station. He was wearing his sharp suit and posh shoes, and she wished she'd thought to dress up a bit, too, instead of being her usual scruffy scientist self.

'Hi,' she said, suddenly shy now she was with him.

'Hi.' And now he looked equally ill-at-ease.

What now? They weren't *officially* dating, so she could hardly greet him with a kiss. But this wasn't just business any more, either. There was definitely something personal.

'Shall we, um…?' She gestured to the platform, where the train was waiting.

He didn't hold her hand on the train. He didn't hold her hand on the way to the butterfly house, either. And he didn't look that impressed as they walked up to the very ordinary glasshouse. Well, he was an architect who specialised in glass. Of course a square building with a gable roof would be dull and functional, in his view.

Then again, this was the man who'd built a removable glass wall between his house and his garden, and yet his garden was the dullest and most minimalist in the universe. So, the way she saw it, he really didn't have the right to be picky about this place.

'Don't judge it from the outside,' she said.

'Uh-huh.' His expression and the tone of his voice were both firmly neutral.

She'd just have to hope that the inside of the building would work the same magic on him as it did on her. Without comment, she opened the first set of doors and ushered him inside, before closing the doors behind them. And then she opened the inner doors.

She'd timed it deliberately: this was the afternoon lull, when the younger children had gone home for a nap and the older children were still at school, so she and Hugo had the whole building to themselves. The glasshouse was filled with large ferns and tropical plants; dozens of butterflies flitted through the air, a mix of sizes and shapes and glorious colours.

She stopped by one of the feeding stations, primed with slices of banana and pineapple and melon; huge owl butterflies had settled on the fruit and were feeding on the sugar.

'That's impressive,' he said.

Yes, but it wasn't the bit she hoped would really attract him. 'Come this way,' she said, taking his hand.

They passed several Zebra Longwing butterflies that were settled on the greenery, idly flapping their long, black-and-white-striped wings.

'I didn't realise that butterflies could be that shape,' he said. 'They're more like a dragonfly than a butterfly.'

'They're the *Heliconius* type,' she said. 'You'll see other butterflies in here that are the same shape, but with splashes of red on their wings; they're the Postman.'

'Postman because they're red, like a post box?' he guessed.

'No, because they do a daily "round" of their flowers—like a postman delivering letters.'

His eyes lit up. 'That's brilliant. And that one over there's really vivid. I had no idea that butterflies could be lime green.'

'That's a Malachite,' she said. *'Siproeta stelenes.'*

She knew she was babbling, just naming things for him, but it was the only way she could cope. Hugo Grey made her head feel all mixed up.

She took a video on her phone of one of the butterflies hovering above a flower, switching the recording to slow motion mode so she could show him something later that she hoped would amaze him, then continued to walk through the butterfly house with him.

His fingers suddenly tightened round hers. 'The big blue butterflies I remember Rosemary showing me: there's one flying over there in the corner.'

'A Morpho.' The thing she thought—*hoped*—might make the difference. 'Stand still,' she said, 'because they're really curious and they'll come over to have a closer look at you.'

'Seriously?'

'Seriously.'

He did as she suggested, and she watched his expression as one of the butterflies flapped lazily over to them, its wings bright iridescent blue, then landed on his arm. His eyes were full of wonder; all the cynicism had gone from his face. At that moment, it felt as if he lit up the whole butterfly house for her. It was the sweetest, sweetest feeling. As if they were sharing something special. Something private. Their own little world.

'You can breathe, you know,' she said softly. 'You won't hurt it.'

'That's just…' He shook his head, clearly lost for words.

She couldn't resist standing on tiptoe and brushing her mouth against his.

He froze for a moment; and then, as the Morpho flew away again, he wrapped his arms around her waist, returning the kiss. She slid her arms round his shoulders, drawing him closer. And then he really kissed her, teasing her lips with his until she leaned against him and opened her mouth, letting him deepen the kiss. All around them, butterflies flapped their iridescent wings, and she closed her eyes, letting all her senses focus on the feel of Hugo's mouth against hers.

When he finally broke the kiss, she opened her eyes, startled.

'Sorry,' he said. 'I shouldn't have done that.'

'Sorry,' she said. 'Blame it on the butterflies—the excitement of seeing the blue Morpho.'

'Absolutely,' he said.

She was lying; and she was pretty sure he knew it. She was pretty sure he was lying, too. But she had no idea what they were going to do about this. She hadn't felt this attracted to someone for years; but at the same time she didn't want to put the butterfly house project in jeopardy. How did she deal with this, without making a huge mess of things?

'Come and see the pupae,' she said, and slid her hand through the crook of his elbow—just to steer him towards the right place in the butterfly house. It had absolutely nothing to do with wanting to touch him. Though, when he drew her a tiny bit closer, it made tingles run down her spine.

'They're in a box?' He stared at the wooden box with its lines of horizontal canes.

'It's a puparium—the safest place for them to hatch.'

'And they're stuck to the canes?'

She nodded. 'So, once they've wiggled out of the chrysalis, they can hang freely to let their wings dry and fill with blood, ready for flying. In a set-up like this, they might hatch overnight and they'll be let out in the mornings when they're ready to fly. Then they look for a mate and start the courtship ritual…'

Just as she and Hugo were doing. Of sorts. Holding hands. Kissing. Making eye contact, and shying away again, because both of them were so unsure about this whole thing. She felt the colour seep through her cheeks and she couldn't quite look him in the eye. 'The females lay the eggs, and the cycle starts all over again: egg, caterpillar, pupa, butterfly.'

He looked thoughtful. 'It's hotter than I expected in here.'

Did he mean literally or figuratively? It felt hot in here for her, too. Especially when he kissed her. She pulled herself together. Literally, she reminded herself. 'It's the right temperature and humidity for the plants and the butterflies.'

'And it's noisier than I expected, too.'

'That's the air heating,' she explained.

'Maybe we could look at different ways of heating,' he suggested.

Which sounded as if he was thinking seriously about the possibilities of building the butterfly house. Maybe she hadn't ruined everything with that kiss, after all.

'This place is magical. It's a bit like walking through a summery snow globe crossed with a rain forest,' he said.

Did he have a picture of that in his head? Something perhaps that he could do with her project?

'I know a dome wouldn't work, but have you any other thoughts?'

He shook his head. 'Maybe we could have a domed roof. A cylindrical building, with arched windows.'

'Like the ones in the Palm House?'

'That could work.'

If she put the butterfly house first, maybe afterwards she and Hugo could explore what was happening between them.

What was it about this place? Hugo wondered. He'd mused earlier that it was like walking through a summery snow globe. But it wasn't just the brightly coloured butterflies that made it feel so magical; it was Alice, too. There was something special about her. The way she made him feel—with her, for the first time in so very long, it felt as if there was a point to life. As if he was doing more than just existing and trudging from minute to minute. As if her warmth and sweetness had melted the permafrost where he'd buried his heart.

He'd been the one to break the kiss and call a halt. She'd backed off too, blaming it on the butterflies. But it wasn't the real butterflies that had caused that kiss: it was the metaphorical ones in his stomach. The way she made him feel, that swooping excitement of attraction and desire.

What would happen if he kissed her again? Would she back away, skittish as one of her butterflies?

Then he realised that she was speaking.

'Sorry. Wool-gathering,' he said. 'You were saying?'

She was all pink and flustered, and he wanted to draw her into his arms.

'If you're not busy, I could cook dinner tonight. Show you some more butterfly things.'

Was this Alice's way of acknowledging this thing between them and admitting that she'd like to get closer, but was wary at the same time?

That was exactly how he was feeling, too. Wanting to get closer, but scared.

Baby steps.

Starting with dinner.

'I'd like that,' he said.

The pink-and-flusteredness went up a notch. Good. Because she made him feel that way, too.

The Tube was too crowded for them to talk on the way back to her place. Then she went quiet on him during the walk from the station to her flat in Shadwell, which turned out to be in a modern development overlooking a quayside.

'It's a fair bit smaller than your place,' she said, 'but it's home.' She gave him a wry smile. 'Though I do envy you your garden. The nearest I have is a window box of herbs.'

'But you get a view of the water,' he pointed out.
'I guess.'

He realised that her assessment was right when she opened the front door and ushered him inside; her flat really *was* compact. 'The bathroom's there if you need it,' she said, indicating a door off the hallway, then led him into the living room.

There was a bay window with space for her desk and a small filing cabinet; the rest of the room was taken up by a small sofa, a bistro-style table and two chairs, and a floor-to-ceiling bookcase stuffed with books. The walls were all painted cream, but there were strategically placed framed artworks; some were old-fashioned botanical prints of butterflies, and others were small jewel-like modern pieces. And how very different it was from his own stark and monochromatic home; her flat was full of colour and beauty.

'Is that Van Gogh?' he asked, gesturing to a framed poster.

She nodded. 'It's his *Butterflies and Poppies*. They're Clouded Yellows. I saw the original with my best friend—she's an art historian, and she wanted to go to the Van Gogh museum in Amsterdam to see their collection because he's her favourite painter.' She smiled. 'Ruth also took me to the gardens at Giverny, because she's a huge Monet fan. She was waxing lyrical over the bridge and the lily pond, and there I was on the hunt for butterflies. I guess we're as nerdy as each other.'

'My best friend's nerdy, too. He's got this passion for Regency doors, and whenever we go anywhere he's always darting off to take a photograph. His Instagram's full of shots of fanlights and door knockers.' Kit was one of the few people Hugo saw regularly—but a couple of months back Kit and Jenny had invited one of her single friends over to dinner to make up a foursome, and it had annoyed Hugo to the point where he'd pleaded a headache and left early. Things had been a bit strained between them since then; he knew Kit meant well, but he really didn't want to be set up with a suitable woman.

Yes, he was lonely and miserable. Stuck. Things weren't getting better; the more time passed, the lonelier he felt, and the more aware he was of things he and Emma hadn't had the time to do together. All that stuff about time being a great healer was utter rubbish. He was just *stuck*.

Emma would be furious with him.

He was furious with himself.

But he didn't know how to get unstuck again.

Alice was the first person in a long time who'd made him feel connected with someone. He'd probably spent as much time in her company during the last week or so as he'd spent with anyone else outside the office in the previous six months, apart from his parents and Rosemary. But he couldn't expect her to help push him out of his rut. That was too much to ask from someone who'd known him for less than a month—especially as he'd been at odds with her for more than half that time.

'Can I help with dinner?' he asked instead.

'No, you're fine,' she said with a smile. 'My kitchen's a bit on the small side.'

He could see that for himself from the doorway. It was practically a galley kitchen, with just enough room for a cooker, fridge, and washing machine. He noticed that there was a large cork board on the wall with photographs and postcards pinned to it; it was perfectly neat and tidy, but the personal touches made her flat feel like a home rather than just a place to live, as his own house was.

'Let me grab you a glass of wine,' she said. 'Red or white?'

'I ought to provide the wine, as you're making dinner,' he said. And then he was cross with himself. Why hadn't he thought of that earlier?

She flapped a dismissive hand. 'It's fine. Red or white?'

'What goes better with dinner?'

She tipped her head on one side as she considered it; yet again, he was struck by how cute she was. 'White,' she said. 'Though, before I start cooking, do you have any food allergies or are there any particular things you hate?'

'No allergies and I eat most things,' he confirmed.

The kitchen was definitely too small for two people to work in, because she accidentally brushed against him when she took the wine out of the fridge. He almost wrapped his arms round her and kissed her again, but he held himself back. Just.

'Can I do anything? Lay the table?' he asked instead.

She took cutlery from a drawer. 'You can lay the table and then come back for the salad, if you like. Then feel free to amuse yourself with the TV or whatever.'

He laid the bistro table; when he came back to collect the bowl of salad and his glass of wine, she was busy chopping mushrooms and boiling water in a pan. He could smell something delicious; funny, it had been so long since he'd noticed food. He'd seen it as nothing more than fuel ever since Emma had died.

Rather than bothering with the television, he glanced through the books on Alice's shelves; there were some very academic tomes on ecology and butterflies, and a few glossy coffee-table-type books with gorgeous shots of butterflies, mixed in with a smattering of crime novels. There were also photographs on the shelves; the young child was recognisable as her, with an elderly couple he assumed were her grandparents. The graduation photos of Alice were at Oxford and London, with a couple who were obviously her parents. There was another picture of her wearing a bridesmaid's dress, with her arm wrapped around the bride: obviously a close friend, maybe the one she'd mentioned going with to Rome and Amsterdam and France.

And how very different this was from his own house; he didn't have any photographs on display at all. They were tucked away for safekeeping, along with his memories. Where they didn't hurt.

A few minutes later, Alice came in carrying two bowls of pasta. 'Fettuccine Alfredo,' she said. 'I hope that's OK with you.'

He joined her at the table. 'This is lovely,' he said after his first taste.

She inclined her head in acknowledgement of the compliment. 'Thank you, but it's just a very simple pasta dish, not something I've slaved over for hours and hours.'

'It's still lovely,' he said.

Strangely, given that they were in her flat, her space, she'd gone all quiet and shy on him. Hugo had the feeling that, even though Alice had fought like a tigress for Rosemary's butterfly house and she teased him, there was also something about her that was as fragile as the butterflies she studied. A vulnerability that she kept hidden.

'Who are the people in the photographs?' he asked, hoping to draw her out a bit more.

'The one of me when I'm small is with my grandparents, the graduation photos are with my parents, and the wedding is when my best friend Ruth got married last year,' she said, confirming his guesses.

'Nice pictures,' he said.

'Thank you.' She looked at him. 'You didn't have any art or photos in your house. Have you only just finished the renovations?'

'No. I've been there for just over two years,' he admitted. 'I finished the renovations last summer.' He just couldn't face putting up photographs which underscored the hole in his life, or the pictures Emma had chosen, because just looking at them made him miss her.

To his relief, she didn't push him to explain; she merely topped up his glass of wine and then turned the conversation to something much lighter.

And how good it was to spend time with someone else. It made him realise he should've made more of an effort with the people around him instead of trying to hide away from the world and lick his wounds in silence.

After dinner, she let him help with the washing up, then offered him a coffee. 'Though I don't have a fancy machine or fancy glass cups like yours,' she said. 'The best I can do is a cafetière and a mug.'

'A mug with butterflies on it, I presume,' he said, trying for lightness.

'Of course,' she said, and proceeded to make a cafetière of coffee. 'Oh, and I meant to show you the film I took earlier.' She put the mugs on the table, found the film on her phone, and handed it to him.

A black and red butterfly was flapping its wings frantically; and then suddenly it went into slow motion. The two upper wings flapped completely separately from the bottom pair of wings, he realised. 'It looks like a swimmer.'

'Doing the butterfly stroke,' she said. 'Isn't it incredible?'

'When it's at normal speed, you just see the mad flapping. But this—it's really amazing.'

She looked pleased. 'I thought you'd enjoy it.'

And there it was: the warmth and sweetness that had been missing from his life for so long. He wanted more of this in his life, but he was so out of practice at dating. He wasn't sure how to reach out to her. Then again, even if he did reach out to her, and even if Alice responded—could he take the risk of falling in love again, and losing her? Intellectually, he knew that the chances of losing her in the same way he'd lost Emma were tiny; but emotionally the fear of going through all the pain and loss again thudded through him, making him want to back away and keep what was left of his heart safe.

He drained his coffee and said, 'I'd better let you get on with your evening.'

'Of course,' she said, all calm and professional; but Hugo had seen the hurt in her eyes before she'd masked it, and felt guilty.

He didn't mean to make her feel bad. But he couldn't explain, either, not without things getting a whole lot more awkward.

'Thank you for dinner,' he said. 'I'll, um, catch you later.'

'Sure,' she said. 'Thanks for coming to the butterfly house.'

And all the way home Hugo kicked himself. Why hadn't he just opened up to her, admitted that he liked her and wanted to see her but he was scared about things going wrong? Why hadn't he been honest about Emma? Alice had made him feel amazing, that afternoon. And the moment when he'd kissed her and she'd kissed him back…

He was an idiot for not kissing her again. For not asking her out properly. For not taking the risk. Life was too short to spend all your time hiding.

He'd call her tomorrow, he decided. Apologise for being rude. Explain.

And he'd just have to hope that she'd listen.

Alice scrubbed the coffee pot clean. And then she scrubbed it again, because it gave her something to do.

What a fool she was. Why on earth had she thought it was a good idea to cook dinner for Hugo? Just because he'd kissed her in the butterfly house and made her feel amazing?

Then again, maybe it was better that he'd realised this early on that she didn't fit into his world. He'd seen her for who she was: and she simply didn't measure up. Further proof that Barney and his cronies had been right all along and it was what you looked like, what you sounded like, that was most important.

She'd just have to hope that she hadn't jeopardised the butterfly house project with her stupidity.

CHAPTER SIX

ALICE SENT HUGO a text with a butterfly fact on Thursday morning, hoping that she could find some way back to the working relationship they'd established, but there was no reply.

Until her phone pinged almost at the end of the day.

Sorry. Tied up in meetings all day. Fact for you: glass isn't a solid.

It wasn't a liquid or a gas, either. And that statement was definitely an opening. She could ignore it; or she could give in to temptation and reply.

So what is it?

Amorphous solid—molecules can still move inside it, but too slowly for us to see.

He was still playing the nerdy facts game with her, then; but it didn't feel quite as reassuring as

nd her, feel her warmth melting the perma-
st around his heart. But that would involve
blanations he didn't want to give right now,
he duly smiled and escorted her into the ca-
dral. 'We've actually got a slightly different
r. Maybe we'll come back another day and
show you the dome. Today we're focusing on
aircase.'

I owe you for my ticket,' she said.

He shook his head. 'My idea, my bill.'

Then I'm buying coffees and sandwiches
er,' she said firmly. 'No arguments.'

They were just in time to join the tour, and
en they got to the end of it—the bit he'd re-
y been waiting for—Hugo watched Alice's
e, pleased to see how amazed she was by the
an's Stair.

It's a spiral staircase, but it doesn't have a col-
n in the middle,' she marvelled. 'I don't get
v it just floats in the air like that, without fall-
over.'

It's cantilevered,' he said. 'Each step is shaped
it can bear the weight of the next. And it's not
ng to fall over—it's been there for more than
ee hundred years.'

He held her hand all the way to the top, pleased
t she seemed to enjoy the elegant stonework
l wrought-iron railings as much as he did.

What a view,' she said at the top, looking down

she would've liked. Especially as he'd left her
house so abruptly, the previous day.

OK, so he'd made it clear that he didn't want
to take their relationship further. But that didn't
necessarily mean he was giving up on the butterfly house project. She just needed to try and keep
things light and easy between them.

Friday was Emma's birthday and Hugo woke with
a ball of misery in his stomach. He headed for his
office early, but keeping busy didn't help. If he
was honest with himself, he wasn't keeping busy,
either; he was just staring out of the window at
the river. Stuck. Miserable as hell.

Life moved on, so why couldn't he?

Then his phone chimed to signal an incoming
text. He knew before he looked at the screen who
it would be from: Alice.

Your butterfly fun fact of the day: butterfly wings
are transparent because they're made of chitin,
the same protein as an insect's exoskeleton.

Funny, she was the one person he felt he could
handle communicating with today. Probably because she didn't know what had happened, so
she wasn't going to tread carefully round him
and make things worse. And her text was a really welcome distraction.

She was telling him that butterflies were transparent, but the ones she'd shown him were all different colours. He called her on it.

So how come they look different colours?

Scales. As they get older, the scales fall off and
leave transparent spots on their wings. Except for
a Glasswing, which is transparent to start with.

He could just hear her saying that. And then
she'd find a picture on the Internet to illustrate
her point, and maybe she'd test him to see if he
knew what the butterfly was and whether this was
a male or female of the species. He really liked
her nerdy streak; it intrigued him and delighted
him in equal measure, and it made him feel as
if the world was opening up around him again,
as if he was stepping away from the oppression
of his heartbreak. Just being with her made him
want to smile.

Right at that moment he really, really wanted
to see her. The only time he felt vaguely normal
nowadays was when he was with her. How crazy
was that? Before he could overanalyse things and
talk himself out of it, he sent her a text.

Are you busy at lunchtime or do you want to
come and see a staircase?

To his relief, she didn't make him
reply. Alice wasn't a game-player. Wh
was what you got.

Staircase at lunchtime is doable. I
back for a seminar at three.

Meet at St Paul's? When's a good ti

Half-twelve?

OK. See you by the main entrance at

And how weird it was that, for the f
day, Hugo felt as if he could actuall
that there wasn't a huge weight on his
ing every breath a shallow effort.

At half-past twelve, he was standi
thedral steps, looking out for Alice
to spot her in the crowd. He lifted a
knowledgement, and his heart gave
when she waved back.

'Thanks for coming,' he said whe
him.

'I'm looking forward to seeing th
she said. 'And I know it's not glass,
you're going to tell me about that, t
tured up to Wren's enormous dome

What he really wanted to do was

at the elegant spiral with the eight-pointed star at its centre. 'I need to take a picture of this for Ruth.'

'The art historian,' he remembered.

She nodded, and snapped the picture on her phone.

And then he heard the cathedral organist start to play. Something he knew well. Bach. A piece Emma had loved and had used to play on the piano he'd given back to her parents, knowing they'd find it comforting. The piece the organist had played at her funeral. And suddenly the weight was right back in the centre of his chest, along with sapping misery.

Something was wrong. Alice didn't know what, but Hugo looked terrible. There were lines of pain etched round his mouth and smudges beneath his eyes. Once the guide had led them back out into the main part of the cathedral, she said gently, 'I think we need coffee and a sandwich. And somewhere nice to eat it.'

'Sure.'

His voice was flat, worrying her further. She quickly bought coffee, muffins and sandwiches at a shop nearby, then shepherded him to a quiet garden not far from St Paul's.

'I had no idea this place even existed,' he said as they sat down. 'Where are we?'

'Christchurch Greyfriars garden,' she said.

'The church was pretty much lost to the Blitz, apart from the tower, but the authorities have kept the land as a garden. The pergolas are full of bird boxes for sparrows and finches. I love this place because it's full of the most gorgeous blue, purple and white flowers.'

'And butterflies.'

Even now, one was skimming past them. She inclined her head. 'Indeed, because a lot of the plants here are nectar-rich.'

'I'm guessing you know a lot of hidden gardens in London?'

She smiled. 'It kind of goes with my job. I need to know where I can take my students on a field trip semi-locally at different times of the year. Here. Have your lunch.' She handed him a cup of coffee and a sandwich.

'Thank you.'

They ate in silence; it wasn't completely awkward, but Alice could see that he was wrestling with something in his head. She had a feeling that talking about whatever was wrong didn't come easily to him. So, when they'd both finished their sandwich and he was staring into his coffee, she reached out to take his free hand. 'I'm probably speaking out of turn here,' she said softly, 'but you look like you did the very first day I met you—lost.'

'It's how I feel,' he admitted. He looked at her

and his eyes were full of misery. 'It's selfish of me, but I wanted to see you today because you don't tread on eggshells round me. You stomp about and you tease me and you teach me things and you...' He shook his head. 'You make me see things in a different way.'

Which was an incredible compliment, but it wasn't what had snagged her attention. 'Why do people tread on eggshells round you?'

He took a deep breath. 'Emma—my wife. It's her birthday today.'

He was married?

But, before she had a chance to absorb that, he continued, 'She died nearly three years ago.'

Widowed, then. And she was pretty sure he wasn't that much older than she was. Her heart broke for him. 'That's rough, losing her so young.'

He nodded. 'She had asthma. After she died, I found out there's something called Peak Week— it's a week in September when allergies and asthma just spike because there's a big rise in pollen and mould, plus the kids have just gone back to school so there are loads of germs and what have you that compromise people's breathing. Emma was a middle school teacher. I was in America giving a paper at a conference when she had a severe asthma attack.'

Obviously in that week in September, Alice realised.

'She called the ambulance and they came straight away, but she collapsed before she even had a chance to unlock the front door. She had a cardiac arrest and she never regained consciousness.' His expression grew bleaker. 'I never got a chance to say goodbye to her.'

No wonder he'd looked so lost, that day at the solicitor's. The meeting had been about his great-aunt's estate, and it must have brought back all the memories of his wife's death. She put her arms round him and just held him. 'That,' she said softly, 'is so sad. I've never lost anyone near my own age—the only person I've lost is Grandad, and although he went a bit before his time it still felt in the natural order of things. Your wife was so young. It must've felt like the end of the world.'

'It did. And then in the cathedral just now... the organ music. It was something she played on the piano at home. A piece—' his breath caught '—played at her funeral.'

Music that had brought back everything he'd lost. 'I didn't know Emma,' she said, 'but she mattered to you, so she must've been special.'

'Very.'

'Do you have a photo of her?'

For a moment, Alice thought she'd gone too far; but eventually Hugo nodded and took out his phone. He skimmed through the photos, then handed the phone to her.

It was clearly their wedding photograph, with Hugo in a tailcoat and Emma in a frothy dress with her veil thrown back; they were both laughing, radiant with happiness, while confetti fluttered down around them. Emma was utterly beautiful.

'She looks lovely, really warm and kind,' Alice said.

'She was,' Hugo said. And, although Alice was a very different woman, she had that same warmth and kindness about her. The thing that had been missing from the centre of his life. The thing he'd tried so hard to live without. But he'd just been existing, not living. Putting one foot in front of the other, taking it step by step. It was all he could do, without Emma. On his own, nothing made sense.

'Remember the love, not the loss,' Alice said gently. 'I know it's hard when you're missing someone and want them beside you, when you want to share things with them and you can't— but you can still share things in spirit. When I see the first butterfly of spring, I think of Grandad and I kind of send him a mental phone call. I sit down wherever I am and I talk to him about it, remember times we'd seen that same species together, and it makes things not hurt quite so much. Maybe you need to give Emma a mental phone call. Talk to her. Tell her about your staircases and your glass.'

Hugo's throat felt as if it were full of sand. He couldn't speak, so he just nodded.

'And you can still celebrate her birthday with cake, because that's how birthdays should be celebrated.' She produced two muffins from a bag. 'It's white chocolate and raspberry. I hope that's OK. I'm sorry I don't have a candle to put in it and light, but we can pretend we have candles and wish Emma happy birthday.'

Hugo's eyes stung. He and Alice had kissed. They'd started to get close, taken the first tentative steps towards a relationship. Yet she still had a big enough heart to make room for his late wife and celebrate Emma's birthday instead of putting herself first.

'I'll spare you the singing,' she said. 'But happy birthday, Emma.' She raised her muffin in a toast.

'Happy birthday, Emma,' he said, his voice thick with unshed tears.

And how odd that eating cake and wishing his late wife happy birthday made him feel so much better, taking the weight of the misery off his heart. He really hadn't expected this to work.

'Emma used to make amazing cakes,' he said. It was why he rarely ate cake nowadays; the memories were too much for him.

'Then,' she said, 'if the butterfly house project goes ahead, maybe we can call the cafe after her. Emma's Kitchen. And then she'll be part of it, too, along with Viola and Rosemary.'

How on earth had he ever thought Alice was an ambitious gold-digger who didn't care who she trampled on her path to the top? She was nothing of the sort. She was inclusive. Kind. Thoughtful. This was so much more than he deserved, given the way he'd misunderstood her.

And she still wasn't taking for granted that the butterfly house would go ahead. She wasn't seeing his feelings as a weakness and using them to pressure him into getting her own way. She was being *kind*.

It made him feel too emotional to speak again. He just took her hand and raised it to his mouth, pressing a kiss into her palm and folding her fingers over it. He hoped she understood what he was trying to say. How much he appreciated her being there. How he wanted things to be different.

She rested her palm against his cheek. 'I have half a dozen students expecting me this afternoon, but I can call them now and reschedule our seminar.'

He shook his head. 'That's not fair.'

'It's not fair of me to leave you right now,' she said.

'I have meetings, in any case.' Meetings that

he'd force himself to get through, and he'd do his job well, the way he always did. He had his professional pride. He took a deep breath. 'You've made me feel so much better today. Thank you.'

Her grey eyes were unsure. 'Do you want me to walk you back to your office?'

'No. But I'll walk you back to the Tube.'

'All right.'

She didn't push him to speak on the way back to the station; she just let him be. No wrapping him in platitudes and pity, and he was grateful for that. How often did you find someone who'd just let you be you, with no pressure?

'I'll call you later,' he said.

'OK.' She stood on tiptoe and kissed his cheek. Just once. 'Give that mental phone call a try. It always makes me feel better.'

And then the train pulled up at the station and she'd gone.

Hugo was thoughtful all afternoon, between meetings.

A mental phone call.

Better than that, he'd visit. Just as he always did on Emma's birthday, his own birthday, their wedding anniversary and the anniversary of her death.

He took stocks, her favourite flowers, to the churchyard, and rinsed out the vase on her grave, filling it with fresh water before adding the new flowers.

'Happy birthday, my love,' he said, sitting down next to the grave. 'I can't believe it's nearly three years, now. I miss you so much, still.' He swallowed hard. 'And I know you'd be furious with me for moping. I know I need to move on—to live life to its fullest, the way you used to do. But it's just so hard without you, Em.'

He wrapped his arms round his knees. 'I miss you. And this is incredibly crass of me to say this on your birthday—it's wrong on so many, many levels—but I've been so lost and lonely without you. And I've met someone. She would've liked you, and I think you would've liked her.'

He sighed. 'I'd like to ask her out. I think we could make each other happy. And she's not replacing you—I'll always love you, and I'll always keep your memory alive. She doesn't want to push you out of my life, either; she thinks we ought to call the cafe at the butterfly house after you. This whole thing makes me feel so mixed up. I want to move on, but I feel as if I'm letting you down all over again. If I hadn't gone to that conference...' Would Emma still have been here? Would he have managed to get help to her in time? Or would she still have collapsed and had that heart attack, and the medics still wouldn't have been able to save her and he would still have felt guilty? He blew out a breath. 'Is it selfish of me to want to find happiness again?'

A moment later, a white butterfly landed on the stocks and basked in the sunlight as it fed on the flowers.

Hugo stared at the butterfly. This felt like a sign. As if Emma was giving him her blessing to ask Alice out—and telling him to build the butterfly house.

Emma's Kitchen it was, then.

'I love you, Em,' he said as the butterfly flittered away again.

And now he knew what to do.

'You really do make the best Buddha bowl in the universe,' Alice said, smiling at her best friend as she laid her fork down on the empty bowl. 'Spicy chicken, wild rice and extra avocado. It doesn't get better than that.'

Ruth laughed. 'Indeed.'

And then Alice's phone pinged. Normally she would've ignored a text during dinner, but she noticed Hugo's name on the notification.

'From the look on your face,' Ruth said, 'I'm guessing that's something you need to deal with.'

'I've come to have dinner with you, not be glued to my phone,' Alice said.

'I know, but I'm going to get the ice cream. I

think you can be forgiven for reading a text while I've left the table.'

'Thanks.' Alice opened the message, and frowned.

Can I take you to dinner tomorrow night?

Did this mean that Hugo wanted to talk about the butterfly house?

Then her phone pinged again.

That's a social invitation, not a butterfly/glass discussion. Keeping things separate.

Alice stared at the phone, not sure whether she was more thrilled or terrified.

Unless she was being very dense, Hugo Grey had just asked her on a date.

'Everything OK?' Ruth said, coming back with two dishes, a bowl of raspberries and a tub of caramel ice cream.

'Yes. No.' Alice dragged a hand through her hair. 'I don't know.'

'Spill,' Ruth said.

'It's Hugo.'

'Rosemary's great-nephew, the man you wanted to throttle?' Ruth asked.

'We've moved on a bit, since then,' Alice said. 'We've been talking about the project and having field trips.'

'Field trips,' Ruth said, with a knowing look.

'Not dates,' Alice corrected.

'But?'

Alice squirmed. Trust her best friend to notice the invisible 'but'. 'There appears to have been some hand-holding.' When Ruth didn't say anything, just looked levelly at her, Alice caved further. 'And some kissing.'

'That, honey, doesn't sound remotely like what a field trip should be. It sounds as if you're dating.'

Which was what Hugo was proposing now. Something Alice wanted to say yes to—but she was scared that it would all go wrong.

'It's complicated,' Alice said. 'I send him nerdy facts about butterflies. He sends me nerdy facts about glass.'

'Flirting by nerdiness. That sounds good,' Ruth said. 'It means he gets you. So do I take it that he's just asked you out officially?'

Alice nodded.

'Then say yes.'

'You know how rubbish I am at relationships. I always pick someone who wants to change me. Robin, Ed, Henry —and Barney.' She grimaced. 'Hugo's from the same kind of background as Barney, one where I don't fit in.'

'Maybe it'll be different, this time,' Ruth suggested.

'Maybe it won't.' Alice sighed. 'He's a widower.'

Ruth raised her eyebrows. 'He's a lot older than you, then?'

'No. His wife died tragically young—an asthma episode caused a heart attack.' She swallowed hard. 'I think I'm the first woman he's asked out since she died. Nearly three years ago.'

'And you haven't dated in a year. It sounds to me as if you might be good for each other,' Ruth said.

'What if I get it wrong?'

'Then you get it wrong. But if he's as nerdy as you, in his own way, that's a good thing. You'll understand each other.'

'I just don't want to get it wrong,' Alice repeated.

'What if you get it right?' Ruth asked. 'Then, if you say no, you'll miss out. I know Barney really hurt you, but you're an amazing woman and I'm proud to call you my friend. If you back off from the chance of a relationship, you're letting Barney win—and you're worth more than that.' Ruth squeezed her hand. 'The only way you'll find out is to date him. What have you got to lose?'

Alice bit her lip. 'The whole of the butterfly house project. I can't risk that.'

'What did he say?'

Alice handed her phone over.

Ruth read the texts swiftly. 'He's pretty clear about wanting to keep things separate. He's asking you out for dinner. As a date. Nothing to do with the butterfly house. I think you should say yes.'

Alice looked at her in an agony of indecision.

Ruth tapped in a reply. 'OK. Done.'

'What? Ruth! No! What did you say?' Alice asked, horrified.

Ruth handed the phone back.

'"I'd love to. Let me know where and when,"' Alice read aloud, and groaned. 'Oh, no.'

'Ally, you've admitted that you've kissed him and you've held hands and you've been flirting by text. This is the next step, that's all.' Ruth leaned across the table and hugged her. 'I just want you to be as happy as I am with Andy. I know you don't need a partner to be a valid person, but I worry that you're lonely.'

'I've got good family and good friends—the best, when they don't commandeer my phone and send texts under my name,' Alice said pointedly, 'and good colleagues.'

'Which is not the same as sharing your life with someone.'

Alice's phone pinged with another text.

Pick you up at seven tomorrow.

So it was a definite date. 'Oh, help. What do I do now?'

Ruth had known her for long enough to be able to guess what the issue was. 'Ask him where you're going,' Ruth said, 'and I'll tell you what to wear.'

Alice duly texted Hugo.

Surprise was the answer.

'That doesn't help at all.' Alice bit her lip. 'What if I wear completely the wrong thing?' Just as she had in Oxford, and Barney's set had all mocked her for it. 'We're talking about a man who wears handmade Italian shoes.'

Ruth smiled. 'It sounds to me like a good excuse to go and buy a new dress.'

'I hardly ever wear dresses.'

'I wish,' Ruth said, 'you'd get over how Barney made you feel. What you wear isn't as important as feeling comfortable in it.'

'And I don't feel comfortable in a dress.'

'Because you can't hide behind a T-shirt slogan, hiking boots and a camera?' Ruth asked, raising one eyebrow.

'The first time I met Hugo, I was wearing a business suit, and I…didn't come across well.'

'Neither did he, from what you told me. It's got nothing to do with what you look like.' Ruth frowned. 'Ask him if a little black dress is appropriate or if he can suggest a dress code.'

'I don't have a little black dress.'

'I do,' Ruth said, 'and you're the same size as me, so there are no excuses. Text him.'

Alice knew if she didn't, Ruth would simply steal her phone and do it for her, so she gave in and texted him. When her phone pinged, she read the text. 'He says wear whatever I like, but a little black dress would be just fine.'

'It's you he's dating, not your clothes,' Ruth said. 'I like the sound of that. It's a good thing. Make that leap of faith, Ally. He's not Barney.'

'But I already told you, he's from the same kind of background as Barney,' Alice pointed out. 'The kind of people who judge me and find me wanting.'

'You're a woman who has three degrees and a heart as big as the world: in what *possible* way can you be found wanting?' Ruth asked.

The answer to that was burned into Alice's heart. She'd learned that from Barney and his friends and their mocking laughter. 'The wrong background. The wrong clothes. The wrong manners.'

'Anyone who's that shallow isn't worth your time,' Ruth said. 'And not everyone from that background is like Barney. You've just always chosen Mr Wrong.'

'So what makes Hugo any different?'

'That,' Ruth said, 'is for you to answer. And

the only way you're going to find the answer is to date him.'

Alice couldn't really reply to that.

'Now stop fussing and eat your ice cream,' Ruth said, 'because we have a dress to sort out.'

Working on Viola's journals, her current favourite part of her job, didn't manage to calm Alice's nerves, the next day.

Would dating Hugo Grey turn out to be a huge mistake?

Even if he didn't hold her background against her or want to change her, there was the fact that he'd lost his wife in such tragic circumstances. How could she ever measure up to the love of his life?

With her borrowed dress, the shoes she'd worn the first time she'd met Hugo, and the butterfly necklace her parents had given her for her thirtieth birthday, she felt polished enough to cope with wherever he was taking her. Though, when the doorbell rang, she had butterflies in her stomach. Stampeding ones. A whole forestful of Monarchs in the middle of a long-distance migration.

'Hi. You look lovely,' he said.

'Thank you. So do you.' And her voice *would* have to go all squeaky, wouldn't it?

Hugo looked gorgeous in a dark suit that she

would just bet was custom-made, teamed with a crisp white shirt and an understated silk tie… and yet another pair of handmade Italian shoes. The man was a walking fashion-plate. And, although it would normally have made her worry that she wasn't stylish enough, the way he looked at her—the heat in his eyes, the way he was smiling just for her—made her feel special. The fact that a man as gorgeous and talented as Hugo had called her 'lovely' made her feel as if she were walking on air.

'For you,' he said, handing her a bouquet of delicate flowers in shades of blue and cream—cornflowers, cream-and-pink-swirled Californian poppies, honeysuckle and columbines.

'Thank you. They're beautiful,' she said.

'I asked the florist for something different, because I didn't think you'd enjoy hothouse blooms. And you said you liked blue flowers.'

'I do.' And she loved the fact he'd made such an effort, instead of grabbing the first bouquet he saw. There was real thought behind this. Substance, not just style. She breathed in the scent of the honeysuckle. 'These are so lovely. I ought to put them in water before we go. Have we got time?'

'Sure.'

'Come in.'

The cornflowers were almost the same shade

of blue as his eyes, and it made her smile. She put the flowers in water and stood the vase on the kitchen windowsill. 'They're perfect. Thank you.'

'Pleasure.' He smiled at her. 'Are you OK to walk in those shoes?'

'I didn't think my hiking boots would quite go with this dress,' she said, aiming for lightness.

'Perhaps not. I thought we'd get the Tube to the restaurant, then maybe have a walk along the river and get a taxi back, if that's OK with you?'

'That'd be nice,' she said, wondering just how flashy the restaurant was going to be and how out of her depth she was going to feel.

But, when they arrived at the restaurant, it was nothing like she was expecting. The waitress led them to the rooftop where there were several glass pods, all containing pots of enormous ferns decked with fairy lights as well as tables and chairs. Most of the pods were already full but there was one clearly waiting for them.

'We're eating in one of these glass pods?' she checked.

'I thought it might be nice to have a view of the sunset over the river,' he said. 'Is this OK with you?'

'It's more than OK,' she said. A glass dome— his favourite thing—plus beautiful plants and a view of the sunset. It was the perfect first date.

Once they'd ordered and the waitress had

brought them a bottle of wine, he said, 'When I asked you to dinner, last night, I wasn't sure if you'd say yes.'

'I wasn't sure, either,' she admitted. 'You're still grieving for Emma.'

'But I need to move on. And you're the first woman I've really noticed since she died.' He took a deep breath. 'I took your advice.'

'The mental phone call?'

He nodded. 'I went to her grave. I talked to her about you, and about how I'd like to ask you to dinner. And I'd just finished talking when this white butterfly settled on the flowers I'd taken with me. It felt like a sign. So I texted you when I got home.'

'I was at my best friend's,' Alice said. 'Actually, this is her dress. I, um, don't often wear dresses.'

'Because of the ticks?'

So he remembered what she'd said. That made her feel a lot more confident. 'Something like that. So what does an architect do in his spare time?'

'Work,' he said. 'Make calculations.'

Which sounded very lonely, to her.

'What does a lepidopterist do in her spare time?' he asked.

'Have dinner with friends, go to the cinema, and visit art exhibitions with my best friend—on condition she visits an SSSI with me.'

'A Site of Special Scientific Interest?' he asked.

She nodded. 'When I'm planning a field trip for my students, I scope it out first. So Ruth and I have a girly road trip.'

'Like our field trips?'

'Something like.' She looked at him. 'This is odd. Being here together, not talking about the butterfly house project.' The thing that scared her. 'Actually on a date.'

'On a date.' He met her gaze head-on. 'You know why I haven't dated since Emma died. You told me you're married to your job. Why don't you date?'

Oh, help.

She didn't want to tell Hugo about Barney. About how pathetic and worthless she'd felt when she'd learned the truth about why Barney was really dating her. How pathetic and worthless she still felt, thanks to the men she'd dated since. 'Let's just say I'm not great at picking Mr Right.'

But he didn't let her weasel out of answering his question.

'What normally makes them Mr Wrong?' he asked.

She'd soon find out if he was another of them, so she might as well be honest. 'They want to change me,' she said simply.

He frowned. 'You're supposed to date someone because you like them and you want to get to know them better, not because you want to make them into someone else.'

That was reassuring. 'How do you get to know someone better?' she asked.

'Search me. I'm out of practice,' he said. 'Emma and I met at university, in our last year. Friend of a friend at a party sort of thing. We just clicked, and I never looked at anyone else after that.'

She blinked. 'Are you telling me this is your first "first date" since you were twenty-one?' She wasn't sure whether that made her feel special— or scared that she wouldn't live up to his expectations.

'Yes. So I'm a bit out of practice.' He grimaced. 'I apologise if I'm making a mess of it.'

So was he feeling as nervous as she was? Wanting to reassure him, she said, 'You're not. Whereas I have a PhD in making a mess of first dates. The wrong clothes, the wrong conversation...' She shrugged. 'The wrong everything.'

'Maybe,' he said, 'we shouldn't call this our first date.'

Because he'd already seen enough of her to change his mind? Because she'd crashed and burned yet again?

Her thoughts must've shown in her expression, because he added quietly, 'To take the pressure off both of us. This is dinner between people who might become friends—and who might become something else.'

'So it's a getting-to-know-you sort of thing.' Which was a lot less scary. At his nod, she said, 'As a scientist, I get to know things by asking questions.'

'Go for it,' he said.

She'd start with an easy one. Something that didn't have any real emotional investment. 'What's your favourite food?'

'Cheese. Really salty, crumbly, strong Cheddar, with oatcakes and a glass of good red wine. You?'

'Parkin, like my gran makes,' she said promptly, 'with a cup of proper Yorkshire tea. Strong.'

'So *that's* your accent,' he said. 'I wasn't sure.'

She tried not to flinch. 'Just so you know, I'm proud of being from South Yorkshire.' Even though Barney's crowd had sneered at her heritage. *The lass from t'pit. The oik.*

'And so you should be. Yorkshire's given us Yorkshire pudding, the Brontës and Wensleydale cheese. Kit—my best friend—is from York,' he said.

'My best friend's a Cockney,' she said. 'We have fights about whether London or Yorkshire is better. Our last fight was traditional dishes— jellied eels versus parkin.' She spread her hands. 'I won that one. No contest.'

'Jellied eels are definitely not my thing. Though

I couldn't judge fairly, because I've never eaten parkin,' he said.

'Even though your best friend is from York-shire?' At his nod, she said, 'Then I'm taking that as a challenge.'

'Good,' he said, 'because tonight might not be our first date—but as far as I'm concerned I don't want it to be our last.'

She was glad of their food arriving, because she didn't have a clue what to say next. The pos-sibilities of where they went from here had com-pletely flustered her.

'OK. So you like the sweet stuff and I'm more savoury,' he said. 'Music?'

'Whatever's on the radio. Though at Christ-mas I like proper carols, like they sing at home.'

'Kit made me go to a folk festival with him in Yorkshire, when we were students.' He grinned. 'Beforehand, I was planning to tease him about brass bands and Morris dancers—except I abso-lutely loved the music. And the beer was really good.'

'So you like live music?'

'Pretty much anything,' he said. 'Not super-heavy classical, though I've been to a few proms with Em.'

'Ruth and Andy had an amazing group at their wedding. Quartus. A string quartet which played a mix of popular classical music and pop—it was really romantic,' she said.

'You like dancing?'

She had—until the ball where she'd learned the truth about Barney. That had put her off. Though telling Hugo the whole truth made her feel too ashamed. 'I'm not very good at it,' she said instead. 'You?'

'I have two left feet. I can't do much more than sway, and even then I might not do it to the right beat,' he admitted.

So far, they seemed compatible. 'What kind of thing do you read?' she asked.

'Background reports on architectural projects,' he said. 'Strictly non-fiction.'

'Which explains why you don't have any bookshelves.'

He shrugged. 'Em was the reader, not me,' he said.

And books reminded him of her, so he didn't keep them in his house? she wondered. Before she could find the right words to ask him, he said, 'I already know you read scientific stuff about Lepidoptera, have gorgeous photographic books of butterflies, and you read crime novels.'

'Not gory ones,' she said. 'I like the clever ones where you solve a puzzle.'

'So from a scientist's point of view,' he said.

'I guess.' She smiled. 'I don't like gory films,

either. The ones I see with Ruth tend to be art-house movies or costume dramas.'

'Em loved costume dramas. Anything Jane Austen.' He looked at Alice. 'Do you mind me talking about her?'

'Of course not. She was a big part of your life and you loved her. Not talking about her would be weird.'

'You're so easy to talk to,' he said. 'Yet, the first day I met you, you were terrifyingly polished and unapproachable.'

'That was the idea,' she said. 'To look professional, in case the meeting was about Viola's journals and you were on the side that could cancel the project.'

'But that wasn't who you are,' he said.

She went very still. 'Meaning?'

'You're not a suit. You're a scientist. You're about seeing the world in a different way,' he said.

She felt the colour flood into her face. 'That might be the nicest compliment anyone's ever given me.' She could tell he meant it. He saw her for who she was and, although she found it hard to believe this was real, he actually seemed to like her for who she was. 'Thank you.'

'It wasn't meant to be schmoozy—more trying to say that the real you is a lot more approachable,' he said. 'When I found out who you were... I didn't think you looked like a butterfly expert.

Not in that suit. That's why I didn't think you were genuine.'

'Remember what my favourite T-shirt says: "Don't judge a butterfly by its chrysalis".'

'I like that.' He paused. 'I'm glad I'm getting to know you.'

'Me, too.' Even though part of her still worried. Hugo's world was like Barney's. When he got to know her better, would he realise that she wouldn't fit in? Would he change his mind about dating her? Or, worse—despite what he'd said about not wanting to turn someone into something else—once he got to know her better, would he want her to change, the way almost all her past boyfriends had?

The waitress arrived with the food, which was excellent. And thankfully Hugo turned the conversation to food and all the dangerous moments were averted. They watched the sun set over the Thames, the sky looking almost airbrushed and reflecting on the river; after coffee, they walked along the river, holding hands.

'If I was any good at dancing,' he said as they passed a group of people dancing in a fairy-lit square on the South Bank, 'I'd suggest we stop here and join them.'

'Better not. Your posh shoes would be in severe danger,' she said with a smile.

He stopped and drew her close to him. 'But, on

the plus side, if I was dancing with you I'd have an excuse to do this.' He brushed his mouth very lightly against hers.

Heat bloomed through her, and she slid one hand round the nape of his neck. 'There are fairy lights. That's all the excuse you need.'

'I'll remember that,' he said, and kissed her again.

Alice had no idea how far they walked, after that; all she was aware of was the floaty feeling being with him gave her, and the warmth of his fingers twined with hers.

He hailed a taxi to take them back to her flat, and walked her to the front door.

'Would you like to come in?' she asked.

'Not tonight,' he said, and kissed her again on her doorstep. 'But if you're not busy tomorrow, maybe we can have a field trip.'

The heat in his eyes made her ask, 'A field trip or a date?'

'A bit of both,' he said.

'What's the dress code?' she asked.

'Whatever you're comfortable in,' he said, and frowned. 'Why do you worry so much about what to wear?'

Explaining that would open up a can of worms she'd rather leave closed. 'Thinking about ticks,' she said lightly. 'Urban or countryside?'

'Both,' he said. 'Your hiking boots are fine.

And maybe I can cook us dinner tomorrow night.'

So he wanted to spend the whole day with her? 'That would be lovely,' she said. 'Where do you want to meet, and what time?'

'Chelsea Physic Garden at half-past eleven,' he said.

She grinned. 'I notice you've gone for an owl-type hour.'

'It means we can have brunch,' he said. 'See you tomorrow.' He kissed her lightly.

'Thank you for tonight,' she said. 'It was amazing.'

'Good. And tomorrow's mainly a date, by the way,' he said.

She kissed the corner of his mouth. 'I'll look forward to it.'

CHAPTER SEVEN

THE NEXT DAY, Alice was already waiting by the entrance to the gardens when Hugo got there, and his heart skipped a beat when he saw her.

'Hi.' He'd said goodbye to her with a kiss, yesterday. Could he say hello with a kiss, too? He was so out of touch with dating, and he didn't want to get this wrong. It was ridiculous to feel this nervous and awkward; he was thirty-two, not fifteen. But he had a feeling that Alice could really matter to him, and he didn't want to make a mistake that could take all the possibilities away.

She blushed. 'Hi.'

Her voice was slightly breathy and shy, and that decided him. He kissed her cheek. 'Thank you for coming.'

'I really thought we'd be heading to see a dome or a staircase,' she said, and he loved the slightly cheeky, teasing look in her eyes.

He smiled and took her hand. 'The staircase I want to show you next isn't open at weekends. Maybe Wednesday lunchtime?'

'That works for me,' she said. 'So why did you pick here?'

'I used to come here with Rosemary when I was small. I haven't been for a few years,' he said, 'but I wanted to take a look at the glasshouses.'

'Is that what you meant by *mainly* a date?' she asked. 'Are you in the running to restore the glasshouses or something and you wanted to check them out?'

'Possibly, but that's not what I had in mind,' he said. 'Let's go for a wander.'

She handed him a ticket, pre-empting any arguments over who was going to pay for their admission. 'Seeing as I got here before you,' she said, 'and you took me to dinner last night, our admission's on me.'

'It's my idea, so it's my bill,' he protested.

'No. We're sharing,' she said firmly.

He sighed. 'Alice, I've apologised for ever thinking you were a gold-digger. I know you're not like that.'

'Good. But let's not fight,' she said, and tucked her arm into the crook of his.

Strolling round the gardens with her was a delight. She pointed out her favourite flowers, and several different species of butterflies; but, more than that, Hugo just liked being with her. He didn't have to pretend, with her; he could just be himself. She knew about Emma, and she hadn't judged him or told him what he should be doing. Not having to fake being a normal, functioning human being was so refreshing; and, in a weird way, taking that pressure off meant that he could actually function normally and focus on things he usually didn't have the energy to notice because he was too busy trying to get through the day.

When they stopped at the cafe for brunch of coffee and a bacon sandwich, he said, 'I want to run something by you.'

'Is this the non-date part?' she asked.

'Yes.' He paused. 'I've been looking at your figures for the butterfly house.'

She went very still. 'Uh-huh.'

'Tomorrow I'll instruct Philip Hemingford to fulfil my great-aunt's will.' He smiled. 'Though you've probably already guessed that.'

'I hoped you would,' she said. 'But you hadn't actually said you'd build the butterfly house—just that you'd think about it. I'm so glad.'

'Good. We need to revise our planning application,' he said. 'And I can't guarantee they'll say yes.'

'But it's more likely they'll say yes if you've had a hand in it.'

'Not because of who I am,' he reminded her. 'Just that I'd word it in a different way—I know the guidelines of most planning departments and the words that work for them.'

Her eyes filled with tears. 'I'm so glad you're going to do it. But, just to be clear, that isn't why I agreed to date you.'

'Good. I was hoping it was because you wanted to see me for *me*.'

She nodded. 'It is. But what you've just told me—I think you've scrambled my brain, because now I'm…' she spread her hands '…speechless.'

He reached across the table, took her hand, pressed a kiss into her palm and folded her fingers over where he'd kissed her. 'That's one of the things I value about you. What you see is what you get.'

She didn't reply, but her eyes sparkled again with unshed tears.

'I thought maybe I could show you some rough ideas for the butterfly house, later this afternoon.'

'I'd love that,' she said.

And he was looking forward to seeing her reaction. He'd spent half the night sketching, and it was the first time he'd felt really inspired since Emma's death—the first time his designs had flowed instead of feeling mechanical and as if he was simply ticking boxes. It was all because of Alice: without her, he wouldn't have remembered how much it made his heart sing to work with glass, or discovered how amazing a butterfly house was. It felt like coming back into the spring after a very long, dark winter. New shoots everywhere, green starting to soften the bare branches, birds singing madly in the morning. He was starting to get the joy back in his life, and he wanted more.

After lunch, Alice wanted to visit the shop. She emerged with a recyclable shopping bag slung over her shoulder; she didn't say what she'd bought, and Hugo didn't want to be pushy and ask.

'Do you want me to carry that for you?' he asked instead.

She smiled. 'Thank you, but I can manage.'

So instead he held her hand while they crossed the river and walked back through Battersea park, past the rose garden and under the pergola.

'I know it's pretty much past its best now, but the wisteria's still so pretty,' she said. 'I love walking through Kensington in wisteria season.'

He'd never really been bothered about wisteria before, but he couldn't resist kissing her under the pergola, with the lilac blooms hanging down. 'Works for me,' he said with a grin.

Back at his house, he opened the glass wall to the garden.

'Is it OK for me to potter round your garden?' she asked.

'Sure. Have a seat on the patio. I'll make coffee,' he said.

'I brought something to go with it.'

When he'd finished making the coffee, she

was sitting down, looking at something on her phone. It took him another ten minutes to notice that the bag she'd had slung over her shoulder was missing—and there was something in his garden that definitely hadn't been there before. 'There's a pot of flowers in my garden.'

'A *small* pot,' she said.

'Flowers.' That must've been what she'd bought from the shop at the Chelsea Physic Gardens. 'I don't do flowers.'

'They're Leucanthemums—Shasta daisies,' she said.

Big white ones. Flowers he didn't have a clue what to do with.

'They're beginner flowers. You can neglect them and they'll still be fine,' she reassured him, clearly guessing at his concerns. 'They don't mind full sun or partial shade, they're hardy, and they're not fussy about soil type. The main thing is that they're great for pollinators.'

He still couldn't get his head round this. 'You bought me a plant.'

'Call it a garden-warming present.'

'I moved here two years ago.'

'Late garden-warming, then. Because I didn't know you two years ago.'

She'd just put flowers into his very plain outdoor area, showing him he didn't have to be surrounded by plain boxes. Although she'd only moved him a tiny fraction out of his rut, it was enough to make him slightly unnerved. He'd wanted to move on, but now it was happening he wasn't entirely sure he was quite ready for this.

As if he'd spoken aloud, she put her arms round him and kissed him. 'I'm sorry. I'll take it back with me if you really hate it.'

How could she take it with her, when she didn't have a garden? And he was being ungrateful. The gift had been motivated by kindness. 'It's not that I hate it. I'm just not a gardener.' He knew about buildings, about glass and staircases. Even though Rosemary had talked to him a lot about plants when he was young, and his mother was very fond of her outdoor space, Hugo didn't have a clue about how to maintain a garden. Alice had pushed him out of his comfort zone.

'Was Emma the gardener? Because I didn't mean to trample on a sore spot. I'm sorry.'

'We didn't have a garden at our flat,' he admitted. 'And, no, she wasn't really a gardener.'

She looked thoughtful. 'So technically you're a garden virgin.'

Just when he thought he'd worked her out, she said something that threw him. 'Did you just call me…?'

She kissed him again. 'I apologise. But just watch. I promise this will be worth it.'

Ten minutes later, there was a bee buzzing

round the pot of daisies. And, ten minutes after that, there was a butterfly.

'See?' she asked softly. 'The difference one little pot can make. When was the last time you saw a bee or a butterfly out here?'

'Hmm,' he said, refusing to be drawn.

'So now can I see your sketches?' she asked.

'They're indoors.'

She followed him into the kitchen, and he brought out his files and spread the sketches on the table. He'd sketched a cylinder with a domed top, more or less what he'd suggested at Kew. 'The panels on the sides remind me of the Victorian glasshouses we saw at Kew. The ones from Viola's era. This is perfect,' she said. 'There's plenty of space for the plants and the butterflies, as well as the heating system and the puparium.' She looked at him. 'But what *I* think isn't important. What really matters is the planning committee's view.'

'I tweaked your application—*our* application,' he corrected. 'Hopefully we can get outline permission now, then work on the detail later. Have a look at what I've done. If it sounds right to you, I'll submit it tomorrow.'

'OK.' She took a small box from her handbag. 'By the way—parkin. I made some this morning. It'll go nicely with coffee.'

'From your gran's recipe?' he asked.

She nodded. 'Which isn't me trying to fill Emma's shoes by baking stuff. Just that you said you'd never tried it, and it's my turn to bring in departmental goodies tomorrow, so I saved you a bit from the batch I made.'

'Good plan,' he said. He opened the box and tasted the gingerbread. 'Now I know why Kit raves about this. Thank you. It's lovely.' He pulled up a file on his laptop and passed it across to her. 'Here's the revised application. Does this work for you or do you want me to change anything?'

She read through it. 'You've said everything I did, except it sounds slightly different.'

'Little tweaks in the wording, that's all.' He raised his mug of coffee. 'Here's to the butterfly house. And may the planners love it.'

'May the planners love it,' she echoed.

After dinner, Hugo drove Alice home. He kissed her lingeringly on her doorstep, enjoying the warmth of her mouth against his and the feel of her arms wrapped round him, holding him close. He'd been at such a low ebb; and Alice made him feel as if he were slowly coming towards the light at the end of a very long and lonely tunnel.

'I'll see you later in the week,' he said when he finally broke the kiss.

'Staircase or butterflies?' she asked.

'Both, if you've got time,' he said.

'Call me. Wednesdays are always good for me,' she said.

'I'll check my diary and move things around, if need be,' he promised, and kissed her again. 'Wednesday it is.'

He waited until she was safely indoors before going back to his car and driving home. Funny how she'd made such a difference to his life. Her butterflies and the way she encouraged him to talk about glass and staircases made him feel so much lighter of heart. He actually found himself looking forward to the day when he woke up, now, because he knew he'd talk to Alice at some point—even if it was only a brief text exchange of nerdy facts. And how much better that was than the last three years, when he'd been dragging himself from one dismal minute to the next and the struggle had exhausted him.

Back at his house, Hugo sat at the kitchen table with a mug of tea, looking out at the garden. That one bright pot of white daisies made the whole space feel different—as if the garden had a focus. Just the way that Alice herself had brought brightness and focus into his life again.

Could it be that his life was finally changing for the better?

On Wednesday, Hugo took Alice to see the helical staircase at City Hall. 'This is something I wish I'd built. And just imagine this as a butterfly house,' he said.

She looked thoughtful. 'Or the Sky Garden. Thousands and thousands of butterflies. It'd be amazing, like seeing a migration of Monarchs— did you know they sound like a waterfall when they fly on migration because there are so many of them?'

'No, but I can imagine it. I still haven't got over that Blue Morpho landing on me. Or seeing the Swallowtail in the fens.'

'I'd like a mix of butterflies in our house, based on Viola's journals,' she said. 'And I definitely want her drawings of those species on the website. Ruth's husband is a website designer, so I was hoping he might be able to help us out.'

'That'd be great,' he said. 'I was going to check with my father, in case he has any more family papers or photos that would be useful.'

'That would be brilliant,' she said. 'And maybe tonight I can show you where I've got to.'

'I'd like that,' he said. 'We could get a takeaway for dinner.'

'There's a really good Chinese near me,' she said. 'They do the best dim sum ever.'

'Sounds perfect,' Hugo said.'

He kissed her goodbye at the Tube station. 'See you tonight. I've got a late meeting, so would seven be OK?'

'It's fine.' She stole a last kiss. 'See you then.'

* * *

Over the next couple of weeks, Alice and Hugo were busy at work—Alice with marking and exams, and Hugo with a project—but they managed to see each other a couple of evenings a week and spent the weekends at Rosemary's house. Hugo made lists of what needed to be done in the house and which contractors to ask for quotes, while Alice worked out what needed to be done in the garden—which plants would go where, how the re-wilding would work, and which plants and species they needed for the butterfly house. In between, Alice continued to work on the journals and Viola's biography, and Hugo made more detailed plans for the butterfly house, checking sizes and volumes with Alice to make sure it was the right space for the number of butterflies she wanted to keep in the house.

'Some of this we can do ourselves,' Hugo said at the end of the second week. 'Maybe we can talk friends into coming here to wield a paintbrush or do some weeding and planting.'

'Not until we've got the outline planning permission,' Alice said. 'I don't want to jinx anything by starting things too early.'

'Superstitious?' He stole a kiss. 'OK. But maybe we can make a start on tidying the garden. Whatever happens with the planning, that needs to be done.'

'Says the man who doesn't garden,' she reminded him with a smile.

'Just tell me what's a weed and what isn't.'

'I don't necessarily want to get rid of the weeds. They're good host plants for caterpillars.'

'I can follow directions,' he said.

She frowned. 'You'd take directions from me?'

'Where you have more knowledge and experience than I do, of course.' He looked surprised. 'It would be very stupid not to.'

She really, *really* had to stop assuming he would behave like Barney and want to be in charge all the time. 'All right,' she said. 'Maybe I can ask Ruth and her husband to come and help us at the weekend.'

'And I could ask Kit and his wife,' he said.

Meaning they'd be meeting each other's best friends.

It was another step forward in their relationship, letting each other that tiny bit closer.

Would Kit like her? Would Ruth approve of him? What if they didn't like each other? If their closest friends didn't think they were right for each other, there was a good chance that their families wouldn't, either. And Alice didn't intend to repeat her mistake of not being accepted by her partner's friends.

In the end, Hugo arranged for them all to meet at Rosemary's house to spend the day working on the garden, following up with a barbecue at Hugo's house in the evening.

Alice was already busy working in the garden when Kit and Jenny arrived.

'Nice to meet you, my fellow countrywoman,' Kit said, greeting her with a hug. He reminded Alice of her uncles, with his broad Yorkshire accent and his ready smile, and she warmed to him immediately.

She was just making coffee when Ruth and Andy arrived. Once the introductions were done, Alice asked, 'So do you all want a tour of the house and the garden before we start work?'

At everyone's nod, she led them through into the house. 'We're moving Rosemary's study upstairs, and arranging it so it looks like it would've done in Viola's day,' she said. 'The other rooms on the upper floor will be teaching areas and a library. Downstairs, we'll keep the kitchen for making refreshments, though we'll need to tweak it a bit, and the dining room will be the cafe. Rosemary's study will be the shop, and the living room will be an exhibition area.'

'Is that a William Moorcroft tea set on the dresser?' Ruth asked when they were back down in the kitchen.

'It is,' Hugo confirmed. 'And I'll make you a cup of tea in it later.'

'Seriously? You do know it qualifies as artwork in its own right and it's—'

'—worth quite a lot of money,' Hugo finished with a smile. 'Yes. But my great-aunt believed in using things rather than saving them for best.'

Ruth picked up a cup. 'This is stunning. I love the colours. I've never actually touched any of his work before. This is such a privilege.' She smiled at Hugo. 'Thank you.'

In the garden, Alice showed them the areas they were going to tidy up and the bits they were planning to re-wild; Hugo explained where the butterfly house was going to be and showed them the plans.

'This is going to be amazing,' Andy said.

'*If* we get planning permission,' Alice said. 'If we don't…'

Hugo rested a hand on her shoulder. 'Then we'll keep submitting plans until we make it work. And we'll get public opinion on our side—like your crowdfunding thing. Emma's best friend is in PR, so maybe we can talk her into helping.'

Over the course of the day, Alice thoroughly enjoyed working with Kit and Jenny, chatting to them about what she was trying to achieve with the garden. 'I want it to help children to connect with nature, and maybe take some of the ideas back to their school or even their home. Although not everyone has access to the garden—I only have plants on the windowsill of my flat—even a plant in the window can help.'

'I'd like to see more butterflies and bees in our garden,' Jenny said. 'Maybe you and Hugo could come for dinner one night and you can give me some advice?'

'I'd love that,' Alice said.

'I'd love that, too. It might distract her from the guerrilla gardening at my house,' Hugo said.

'Guerrilla gardening?' Ruth asked.

'My neat, square garden seems to sprout a new plant every time Alice visits,' Hugo explained. 'She started with these big white daisies, and then...' He shook his head sorrowfully. 'They just seem to pop up from nowhere. Triffids, the lot of them.'

'He means lavender, salvia and white cosmos. But they're easy to look after,' Alice said. 'Think how many bees and butterflies you've seen in your garden since I sneaked the flowers in, Hugo.' She gave him a hopeful look. 'It would be even better if you had a tiny wild corner.'

'Which translates as unrestrained nettles,' Hugo grumbled.

'And thistles,' Alice added cheerfully. 'Which is why we've got them here in Rosemary's garden. The emerging caterpillars can't travel far so they need good host plants.'

'You're actually making that horrible square of

his into a proper garden?' Jenny asked. At Alice's nod, she beamed. 'Good.'

'You're all ganging up on me,' Hugo mock complained. 'I'm going to make tea. Even though none of you deserve any.'

'I'll help,' Ruth offered.

'Thank you, Alice,' Kit said when Hugo left the garden. 'It's good to have my best friend back. He's been struggling for a while and the only place he seemed to function was at the office, and even there he wasn't happy. Jen and I tried to support him, but nothing we've done seemed to help. We tried to fix him up with one of her friends, to stop him being quite so lonely, but that made things worse, and...' He shook his head sadly. 'We were idiots. Thank you. You've made a huge difference to him.' He paused. 'I assume you know about Emma?'

'I do, and we're going to call the cafe after her—Emma's Kitchen,' Alice confirmed.

Kit looked pleased. 'That's so nice.'

'It must've been so hard for him, losing her like that,' Alice said.

'It broke him,' Kit agreed. 'But I think you're showing him how to put the pieces back together.'

Just as Hugo was doing for her, Alice thought. He was giving her the confidence in herself that Barney and his cronies had taken away.

At the end of the afternoon, they all headed back to Hugo's house for the barbecue.

'That's another pot for my garden, isn't it?' Hugo accused on the train to Battersea, staring at Alice's recyclable bag.

'I can't hear you. It's too loud on the Tube,' Alice said with a grin.

'I can't see a pot,' Jenny said, looking around at everything except Alice's bag.

'Me, neither,' Kit said, putting his hands over his eyes.

'What pot would that be?' Ruth asked.

Andy looked out of the window. 'No pots here, my friend.'

'Oh, for pity's sake. I give in,' Hugo said, rolling his eyes.

Kit and Alice did a fist bump, and everyone laughed.

Back at Hugo's place, Alice added the pot of lavender to the collection she'd started at the sunny edge of the patio.

'That looks amazing—so much better than that boring square of lawn,' Jenny said. 'And look! There are butterflies.'

'Plus the lavender's from Rosemary's garden. It belongs with Hugo—a family legacy sort of thing,' Alice said.

'Agreed,' Kit said. 'Now let's get this barbecue started.'

Kit and Jenny had organised the wine, Ruth and Andy had brought bread and salads, Alice had sorted out puddings and Hugo had bought meat, fish and veggie options. And it was one of the nicest evenings Alice had spent in a while, getting to know Hugo's best friends while he got to know hers.

'I like him a lot,' Ruth said in the kitchen as they were clearing away and making coffee. 'He's one of the good guys. And I like the way he treats you.' She looked Alice straight in the eye. 'I never met Barney, but I know his type. Hugo isn't like that.'

'I know,' Alice said.

'Barney?' Jenny asked.

'Ally's ex from her undergraduate days. Posh, conceited, selfish, and he treated her badly,' Ruth explained.

Jenny rolled her eyes. 'I know the type, too. Hugo's posh, but not the rest of it. He's a sweetheart. He's had a rough time—but you've made a real difference to him, Alice.'

'It's very early days,' Alice said. 'There are no guarantees.' But she was really starting to hope that this would work out. She liked the man Hugo really was—not the uptight, closed-off man she'd met at the solicitor's, but the architect who loved light and glass and space. The man who understood exactly how she felt about butterflies and listened to her ideas.

They spent the rest of the evening sitting on the patio, drinking coffee and chatting. When the others had left, Hugo walked Alice to the Tube station. 'I liked Ruth and Andy,' he said.

'Good. They liked you, too—and I liked Kit and Jenny.'

He kissed her. 'I'm glad. You made a hit with them, too.'

She stroked his face. 'That's good. I mean, I know dating someone doesn't mean you're dating their friends, but it helps if you all get on.'

'It does indeed.' He kissed her as the train came in to the station. 'See you tomorrow.'

The following weekend, Alice was starting to get antsy. 'It's been three weeks now, and we still haven't heard a thing from the planning people.'

'It doesn't necessarily mean bad news,' Hugo reassured her. 'Holiday season can slow things down.'

'What if they don't give approval?' Alice asked.

'Then we look at the reasons why they rejected the plans and tweak our application to take them into account.' He stole a kiss. 'You can wait for hours to see a butterfly, right? This is the same sort of thing. Be patient.'

She sighed. 'Sorry. I'm behaving like a spoiled brat.'

'No, you just want to get on with things. And we've got everything lined up ready for when we finally get a yes. We've got local businesses whose apprentices need a project to work on, my friend James will do the survey, and Emma's best friend Pavani is a PR specialist and she's getting together a list of possible sponsors to add to the crowdfunding you've already done.' He smiled. 'Why don't we do something tomorrow instead of working on the house or the garden?'

'Such as?'

'Go to the sea,' he said. 'I thought maybe we could go and see a rare butterfly on the South Downs on the way to the beach—the Duke of Burgundy.'

She raised her eyebrows. 'Been researching on the Internet, have we?'

He looked pleased with himself. 'Apparently it's a real conservation success.'

'It is,' she agreed. 'But unfortunately you've just missed the season where the adults fly.'

'How? It's only the middle of July.'

'It's still too late.' She smiled. 'But there are other butterflies we could go and see in Sussex. Marbled Whites, Gatekeepers, maybe a Purple Emperor.'

'You're on. I'll drive,' he said. 'We can see the

butterflies in the morning, paddle in the sea and eat chips for lunch, and have afternoon tea on the way back to London.'

'That sounds like the perfect day,' she said. 'I'd really like that.'

He stole a kiss. 'I'll pick you up at seven-thirty.'

'Are you sure you want to drive? Wouldn't you rather nap in the car?' Just to hammer the point home, she hooted softly at him.

'Sussex isn't as far as Norfolk so we don't have to leave quite so early. I can cope.'

'You're on,' she said. 'Remember sensible shoes and big socks.'

'Yeah, yeah.' His eyes crinkled at the corners. 'Are you this bossy with your students?'

'Absolutely,' she said. 'One of my colleagues was bitten by a tick, some years back. Because she didn't notice the rash, she didn't go to the doctor early enough. Even a month of antibiotics didn't cure Lyme's disease, and she was really ill for a couple of years. It's as debilitating as chronic fatigue syndrome. She still can't work full time, and it's so frustrating for her.'

'Point taken,' he said. 'Sensible shoes, big socks, and I'll see you at seven-thirty.'

CHAPTER EIGHT

HUGO PICKED ALICE up at seven-thirty, as arranged, and they drove to the South Downs. Alice thoroughly enjoyed wandering hand in hand across the footpaths with him, spotting butterflies, and the highlight of her morning was photographing a cluster of Purple Emperors.

'I thought you were teasing about them being purple,' Hugo said. 'They're stunning.'

'Aren't they just?'

From the Downs, they headed to the sea and strolled across the pebbly beach, eating hot, crispy chips.

'I hardly ever go to the sea,' Alice said. 'It's a long way for a day trip. Though when I was small we used to go and stay in Whitby every summer. I'd spend hours beachcombing with Grandad, finding fossils and bits of jet and amber, and we'd eat fish and chips on the cliffs, trying to avoid the seagulls.'

'Living in London, the quickest beach for us to go to was Brighton,' Hugh said. 'I was fascinated by the Pavilion and the pier, but I was always a bit disappointed that the beach was stony. My mother's parents lived in Suffolk, and I loved going to visit them because they lived near this enormous sandy beach and I could spend hours and hours searching for shells and building sandcastles.'

'So what kind of sandcastle does an architect build?' she asked.

'Traditional. Moat, four towers with a flag made of twigs and seaweed, a drawbridge lined with shells, and windows of sea-glass.'

She could just imagine Hugo as a small, intense child, searching for shells and sea-glass to fill his bucket, then making his sandcastle; it made her heart feel as if it had done a backflip.

'So what kind of sandcastle does a butterfly expert build?' he asked.

'Rather less elaborate than yours,' she said with a grin. 'But my gran always went to the beach with flags in her handbag, made from cocktail sticks and pictures she'd cut out of magazines. There were butterflies for me, ponies for my cousin who loved horses, and kittens for my cousin who loved cats.'

'It sounds brilliant,' he said. 'Are you all still close?'

She nodded. 'Grandad's no longer with us, but everyone else is. They all think I'm a bit weird, because I'm the only one in the family who went to uni. My Uncle Jack makes the same terrible joke every single time he sees me about Dr Alice diagnosing someone with butterflies in their tummies, but he doesn't mean any harm by it.'

'It must be nice having a big family,' Hugo said.

'It is. I had a "blink and you'll miss it" spot on a Sunday evening TV programme, last spring. Mum told everyone, and I guess it was a good excuse for a family gathering because she made me come home for the weekend, and everyone came over to ours to watch it and eat cake and drink bubbly.' And Alice had been moved to tears by the pride on their faces as they'd nudged each other and cheered when her face had flashed up on the TV screen.

'That's so nice,' he said.

'I love my family. And I need to make more effort to go up to Yorkshire, because my flat's too small for more than a couple of people to stay at a time.' And maybe, just maybe she could ask Hugo to join her.

Maybe.

Because it was still early days, and she didn't want to get her family all excited at the idea of her finally settling down, when she still didn't know exactly where this thing between herself and Hugo was going.

'So—afternoon tea,' he said when they were back at the car. 'My mother makes the best scones

ever, and my father's got some photos and doc-
uments he thought you might be interested in.'

When it registered with her, Alice went cold.
'We're going to see your parents?'

'For afternoon tea.' He frowned. 'That's OK,
isn't it?

Oh, help. They'd met each other's best friends
and it had been fine, but she wasn't sure she was
quite ready to meet his parents.

'Alice? What's wrong?'

'I, um…just wasn't expecting this.'

'They're not going to give you a hard time
about Rosemary's house,' he said, taking her hand
and squeezing it. 'I was always the one in guard
dog mode, and I'm on your side. Pa's thrilled
about Viola's biography and the journals, and I
know he and Ma would love to hear about your
plans for the garden.'

What would they think of the scruffy scientist
with the messy hair and faded jeans? Hugo came
from a posh family. Would they expect cashmere
and pearls, the way Barney's family had? Alice
remembered the whispers she hadn't been supposed to hear, the disapproval.

*Really, Barney, couldn't you have found some-
one better?*

And, although Alice didn't think that Hugo's
parents would mock her behind her back, the

way Barney's social set had, she was worried that they'd be disappointed in her.

'Uh-huh,' she said, but she was quiet all the way to the village where the Greys lived. And she was quieter still when she realised that they lived in an old rectory—an enormous place at the end of a really, really long driveway.

You don't belong here, oik.

The words echoed in her head, spinning round and round.

'Alice?' Hugo asked.

Belatedly, she realised he'd parked the car. She had no idea what he'd said to her or how long he'd been waiting for an answer.

'Sorry. Bit of a headache,' she fibbed. And then she had to support the lie by hunting in her hand-bag for paracetamol.

With every step across the gravel, she felt worse. An impostor. The girl from t'pit; the oik from the council estate. The Northern version of Eliza Doolittle.

The front door opened and Hugo's parents came out to greet them, a small black and white cocker spaniel with a madly waving tail following at their heels.

'Ma, Pa, this is Dr Alice Walters,' Hugo said.

Right now he sounded even posher than he did in London, and it worried Alice. Was this who Hugo really was?

'So nice to meet you, Dr Walters—or may we call you Alice?' Hugo's mother asked, holding out her hand in welcome to shake Alice's.

'Alice, please,' Alice said.

'I'm Serena, and this is Charles.'

'Pleased to meet you,' Alice said, shaking his hand too.

'And this is Soo.' Serena gestured to the little dog. 'Do you mind dogs, Alice?'

'No, I like them,' Alice said. At least that was one thing they had in common. She bent down to make a fuss of the dog, who immediately threw herself onto her back and waved an imperious paw to indicate that she wanted a tummy-rub.

'I've put the kettle on,' Serena said.

Just as Alice's own mother would have done; that forced the voice in Alice's head, which was yammering that she didn't belong here, to drop down a notch in volume.

'Hello, darling.' Serena wrapped her arms round Hugo, who hugged her back and greeted his father just as warmly.

'I'm so thrilled you're writing Viola's biography, Alice. I always loved those trays of butterflies in Rosemary's study,' Charles said. 'I've been digging through the family archives and I've found some things that might be useful for you.'

Alice noticed that Charles' breathing was a little ragged. Was this what Hugo had meant when he'd said his father was unwell?

'Come and sit down, Alice,' Serena urged. 'It's lovely in the garden right now. Would you prefer tea or coffee?'

'I like both, but please don't feel you have to wait on me. Let me help,' Alice said.

Serena patted her arm. 'Charles is dying to show you what he found. But I'll say yes to some help later.'

This wasn't a rejection, Alice reminded herself. 'OK. Thank you.'

Charles had a box sitting on the table on the patio. 'Viola's letters—that is, letters people wrote to her,' he said. 'I've sorted them into bundles from the writers in date order. I thought they might be useful for the biography, so you can borrow them for as long as you need.'

'Thank you—that's wonderful,' Alice said.

'And there are photographs, some of which might be duplicates of Rosemary's,' Charles added. 'Feel free to use anything that works for the book.'

'That's really kind,' Alice said. 'I didn't re- alise we were dropping in to see you today, or I would've brought my file of photographs for you to look through, too. But I'll be happy to bring them down at any time over the summer.' She glanced quickly through the contents of the box.

'These are wonderful. Thank you so much. I'll credit you with anything I use.'

Charles looked pleased.

Soo was clearly Serena's shadow, and her reappearance heralded Hugo's mother arriving with a tray of tea.

'I'm sorry we didn't meet before, Alice,' Serena said. 'Rosemary clearly thought a lot of you, as she entrusted Viola's biography and journals to you.'

'I thought a lot of her,' Alice said. 'My condolences on your loss.'

'I saw you at the funeral,' Charles said. 'In the background.'

Alice nodded. 'I wanted to pay my respects—but, given what was happening at the time, I didn't want to make things awkward for your family.'

'That's very thoughtful,' Serena said. 'But Hugo's reassured us about what you're both planning to do with the house—turning it into an education centre and a museum.'

'Named after both Viola and Rosemary,' Alice said. 'Though we're still waiting to hear from the planning people.'

'This is what the butterfly house will look like, if the plans go through,' Hugo said, taking out his phone and showing his parents photographs of his sketches.

'The doors remind me of the Palm House at Kew,' Charles said. 'You fell in love with the place when Rosemary took you there. So did I, when I was a boy.'

'So will you have butterflies there all year round?' Serena asked.

'Yes—we'll have tropical butterflies, and we'll buy the pupae from sustainable farmers,' Alice explained. 'The English ones will be in the re-wilded garden during the spring and summer.'

Serena and Charles were interested in everything she had to say about the re-wilding; finally, Serena asked, 'So can you recommend things we can do here to attract more butterflies?'

Hugo groaned. 'Ma, I know where this is going. Don't let Alice talk you into giving her pots of stuff for my garden.'

'If you mean that abomination of a square outside your patio, I'd be more than happy to donate pots of stuff,' Serena retorted.

Alice grinned. 'You're out-womanned here, Hugo.'

'Indeed. Come and see the garden, Alice. We'll leave the men to their tea and we can talk about plants.' Serena stood up, tucked her arm through Alice's, and led her further into the garden.

'At least Charles will sit down and rest with Hugo there to talk to him. He has COPD,' Serena said, when they were out of earshot. 'When he overdoes things he struggles to breathe. And then he gets cross. But will he sit down and rest?'

'That's hard,' Alice said sympathetically. 'My grandfather—the one who was a miner—had emphysema, so I know what it's like.'

'Men never listen.' Serena rolled her eyes. 'I also wanted to thank you, without embarrassing Hugo. It's the happiest I've seen him look in nearly three years, and when he's talked to me about the butterfly house he's been designing for Rosemary's garden it's the first time he's sounded enthusiastic about a project since—' She stopped and bit her lip. 'I assume he's told you?'

'About Emma? Yes, he has,' Alice reassured her. 'It must've been so hard for all of you.'

'It was,' Serena confirmed, looking sad. 'And I've worried about Hugo every day ever since. He shuts himself away, and it's so hard to reach him. There's nothing I can do or say that will help. But you—since he's met you, he's sounded so much better. The light's back in his eyes. He doesn't look defeated all the time.' She grimaced. 'I apologise for being an interfering mother and making him bring you here. I just wanted to meet the woman who's brought my son back into the world again, so I could say thank you.'

'Hugo and I are very different,' Alice warned.

'That's a good thing. It means you'll broaden

each other's horizons instead of living in an echo chamber.'

No censure. No discreetly rolled eyes about Alice having the wrong accent and the wrong background. Here, she was accepted for who she was. Whatever barriers she and Hugo might face in the future, his family wouldn't be one of them. She wouldn't have to pretend she was somebody she wasn't. And it felt as if a huge weight had been rolled off her chest, letting her breathe normally again.

Alice thoroughly enjoyed wandering round the garden with Serena and Soo, making suggestions of dog-friendly plants for particular corners and tiny tweaks that would encourage butterflies and bees.

'I have to confess, I do have a gardener,' Serena said.

Hugo's parents were posh enough to have a gardener?

Maybe Alice's uneasiness showed in her expression, because Serena grimaced and waggled her fingers. 'Arthritis stops me doing as much as I'd like to do, and Charles has brown fingers, not green. And I couldn't bear to be without a garden. So this was the compromise. Jacob lives in the village. He does all the stuff that makes my hands hurt, but he's all about the vegetable patch and he's terribly sniffy about my flowers.' She smiled. 'I had to bully him into letting me have a herb garden. But even he admits that home-made pesto is the best.'

It sounded, Alice thought, as if Serena and her gardener were good friends and bantered together a lot. So it wasn't the same sort of thing as the way Barney's family had looked down on their domestic staff.

'How would Jacob feel about you having a wild corner in the garden?' she asked.

'He'll stomp about, muttering about slugs,' Serena said. 'And we'll have a huge fight about the damage caterpillars would do to the cabbages.'

Alice smiled. 'I'll send you all the figures so you can guilt him into it.'

'Done,' Serena said. 'Now, if you wouldn't mind doing the cuttings yourself, you can have whatever you like for Hugo's garden.'

'Some of your honeysuckle,' Alice said promptly. 'I'd like some for Rosemary's garden as well, please.'

'Of course. Come to the potting shed.' Serena grinned. 'I know where Jacob keeps the spare key. Third stone from the left.'

Alice retrieved the key, and between them they sorted out some pots and some cuttings.

'So Hugo's actually letting you redo his garden?' Serena asked.

'I'm not giving him any choice,' Alice said. 'I

brought lavender from Rosemary's garden, and Kit and Jenny are giving me some plants from their garden next week. That horrible minimalist square is going to be a riot of colour by the time I've finished with it. Kit's going to keep him distracted while Jenny and I sneak in and plant some spring bulbs. He'll complain about it, but secretly he loves it. You can see it in his eyes.'

Serena's eyes filled with tears. 'Emma would have liked you so, so much.' She hugged Alice. 'I'm not going to say any more now. We'll go and make afternoon tea.'

But Alice felt *accepted*. And that made all the difference in the world. Instead of worrying that she was going to say or do the wrong thing, she could relax and just be herself. And it made her hope that she and Hugo really had the chance of a future together.

Serena insisted on both of them taking scones and cake back to London, and the goodbye hug that Hugo's parents gave Alice was very warm indeed.

'Sorry I sprang that visit on you,' Hugo said, once they were out of the village.

'That's the biggest "sorry, not sorry" I've ever heard,' she retorted.

'What, like the one you're about to say about being sorry you raided my mother's garden to put more pots into mine?' he asked archly.

'I'm not sorry about *that* in the slightest,' she said. 'Honeysuckle is one of life's pleasures. If I had a balcony, I'd have a pot of it for there, too.'

He laughed. 'At least you're honest about it.' He paused. 'My parents liked you very much.'

'I liked them, too,' Alice said. And she intended to suggest a field trip to Yorkshire later in the summer so Hugo could meet her family, too. Because now she was confident they'd like each other.

CHAPTER NINE

ON MONDAY, ALICE came home from the university to discover an official-looking envelope in the post. The last time she'd opened an envelope with that particular return address, it had been bad news. Would it be different, this time?

This was so ridiculous. She was far from being a coward, and she'd never been afraid of getting exam results. Then again, she'd always had a good idea how she'd performed in exams. This was all completely out of her control—and of Hugo's. She had absolutely no clue whether the planners were going to say yes or whether the letter would contain another rejection.

She rang Hugo. 'Are you super-busy?'

'Just wrestling with some figures,' he said. 'What's up?'

'I think I've got a letter from the planning people.'

'What does it say?'

'I haven't opened it, yet,' she admitted.

'Why?'

'Because I'm terrified they're going to turn us down.'

'Hang up and I'll video-call you,' he said, 'so then we can open it together. Sort of.'

She ended the call, and he video-called her back.

'Shall I hold the phone so you can see the letter?' she asked.

'For you to show me the whole letter on a phone screen I'd need a magnifying glass to read it this end,' he said. 'Just open it and read it out loud.'

She undid the flap and took out the contents.

'OK. "Dear Dr Walters, Thank you for your revised planning application—"' She stopped, because she couldn't quite take in the next line.

'Alice? Is everything all right?'

'Yes.' Dazedly, she looked at him on the screen.

'Did they say yes or no?'

'They said—' and she still couldn't quite believe it '—yes.'

He whooped. 'Brilliant! We are so going out to celebrate tonight. If you call Ruth, I'll call Kit, and dinner's my shout. I'll call you in ten minutes.'

But when he called back, they both had bad news. 'Jenny's got a work thing tonight.'

'And Ruth's doing a lecture as part of the university's community project,' she said. 'Our celebratory dinner will have to be another night.'

'We'll have two celebrations, then—because I think this sort of news deserves champagne right now. You, me, a takeaway and my back garden tonight?' he suggested.

'OK. You organise the takeaway and I'll bring the champagne,' she said.

'Perfect. What sort of takeaway?'

'Anything. But just remember pizza only comes as thin crust.'

'Pizza and champagne works for me. See you at seven?'

'I'll be there.'

Although she didn't bother dressing up, Alice changed into clean jeans and a T-shirt. At seven precisely, she arrived at Hugo's house with a bottle of champagne she'd bought from the supermarket chiller cabinet and a pot. 'Celebratory scabious,' she informed him, handing him the pot of pink wildflowers.

'You made that up,' he accused.

'Your point is…?' She spread her hands, laughing.

He laughed back, and kissed her. 'It could've been worse, I suppose. Celebratory nettles.'

'Now that's an excellent idea.'

'We've had this conversation. You are *not* filling my garden with nettles.'

'A tiny pond?' she suggested.

'No.' But she noticed he was smiling when he

added the pot to his growing collection. And she also noticed that he had a watering can. A posh metal one, painted green, with a gold-coloured watering rose. She coughed. 'Well, look at that. Been shopping, have we?'

'No. Ma had it delivered to the office this morning, with instructions about how to water the pots,' he said.

'Good, because virgin gardeners should absolutely not choose a watering can without help. Your mum knows what she's doing, so the rose will work.'

'You're putting roses in my garden now?'

'A rose is the thing on the end of the can that does the watering, as I'm sure you know perfectly well. Given that your mum loves her garden and so did Rosemary, I'm calling you on pretending to know a lot less than you really do.'

'Maybe,' he said. 'I like watching you be bossy.'

She had no answer to that, so she kissed him.

There were two glasses and a wine cooler waiting on the patio table; Hugo opened the champagne.

'I want to make a toast,' he said. 'To Viola, who studied butterflies; to Rosemary, who kept all her papers and loved butterflies enough to give us her garden; and to us, because we're going to make the butterfly house happen.'

'To Viola, Rosemary and us,' Alice echoed. 'And to the butterflies.'

After the pizza was delivered and they'd eaten it, followed by the posh salted caramel ice cream and raspberries Hugo supplied for pudding, they continued to sit in the garden, holding hands and talking while the light faded. Finally, Alice started yawning. 'Sorry. My lark tendencies are kicking in. I'd better head for the Tube.'

He met her gaze. 'Or you could stay here to-night.'

Her heart skipped a beat. 'In your spare room?' she checked.

His cobalt-blue eyes were intense. 'Or in my room. With me.'

Stay the night.

Take their relationship to the next level.

Alice wanted to; yet, at the same time, it scared her. This was a big step. They'd gone from hand-holding to dating, to meeting each other's best friends and in her case meeting his family; so far, they'd negotiated all the tricky moments. But this... This was something that could bring them closer together—or it could show just how big the gap was between them.

She didn't think Hugo would deliberately hurt her, the way her exes had, but was he really ready for this? Were they rushing things? Worry made her mouth feel as dry as if they'd been drinking vinegar instead of champagne. She knew she had to be brave and ask the difficult question. 'What about Emma?'

'Emma didn't live here. She never even saw this house,' he said. 'None of the furniture is stuff we chose together. Everything in this house was a fresh start for me.' His fingers tightened briefly round hers. 'You're the only woman I've dated since she died, and the only woman who's been here apart from my mother and a couple of close friends and colleagues.'

She stroked his face, knowing she'd put pressure on a soul-deep bruise. 'Thank you. I just didn't want you to think I'm trying to…' She paused, wanting to find a kind way to say it, except there wasn't one. 'Trying to take her place,' she said in the end.

'I know you're not.' He kissed her lightly. 'And there are no strings. I don't have any condoms, and I don't expect you to have sex with me. But, if you'd like to, tonight I want to go to sleep with you in my arms and wake up with you tomorrow.'

No pressure. No demands. No expectations.

An intimacy that, in some ways, was deeper than just the mechanics of sex.

He'd told her what he wanted. Now she could be brave enough to admit the same. 'I don't have any condoms, either, but I'd like to go to sleep in your arms and wake up with you.'

His kiss was so slow and so sweet that it brought tears to her eyes.

'I'll sort out the laundry overnight,' he said. 'There's a spare new toothbrush in the bathroom. Leave whatever you want washed outside the door, and I'll leave you a T-shirt to sleep in.'

'Thank you.' She loved the fact that he was so organised and so matter-of-fact about things. He'd made it easy.

When she peeked outside the bathroom door, clad only in a towel, there was a plain black T-shirt folded neatly on the floor, large enough to work as a makeshift nightshirt.

Shyness threatened to engulf her, but she put it on and walked into his bedroom.

It was very plain and minimalist, as she'd expected. The bed had a black wrought-iron headboard; the bedding was in tones of blue and grey, matching the curtains. The floor was of sanded boards with a rug next to the bed in the same tones of blue and grey. There was no artwork on the walls, and nothing on top of the chest of drawers except a phone charger.

He was sitting on the end of the bed, looking at something on his phone.

'Thank you for sorting everything out,' she said.

'You're very welcome.' He looked up at her with a smile. 'If you'll excuse me, I'll use the bathroom. Choose whichever side of the bed works best for you. Oh, and just in case you need a phone charger.' He gestured to the dressing table. 'There's a socket either side of the bed.'

She waited until he'd left the room before choosing the right side of the bed and plugging in her phone. Maybe this hadn't been a great idea. Maybe she should've gone home. This was a new level of intimacy, and she wasn't completely sure either of them was ready for it.

Her worries must've shown on her face, because when he came back into the room he sat on his side of the bed, drew her hand to his mouth, kissed her palm and folded her fingers over the kiss. 'No pressure,' he said softly. 'You can use the spare room if you're more comfortable. Or I can.'

'No, I want to. But it's been a while since either of us has done this,' she said.

'It feels weird,' he agreed. 'But I'm glad you're here.'

And that conviction melted some of her worries. 'Me, too.'

He climbed properly into the bed, switched off the light and drew her into his arms. 'No pressure,' he said again.

'No pressure,' she whispered. She brushed her mouth against his, and her lips tingled to the point where she couldn't resist doing it again. And again.

'Alice.' He drew her closer and kissed her back.

Kissing led to touching. Exploring. Discovering where a touch could elicit a sigh of pleasure or a murmur of desire. Her shyness melted away in the dark, and she matched him kiss for kiss, touch for touch.

'I can't do quite everything I want to do,' he whispered, 'but if you'll let me…'

'Yes,' she whispered back, and allowed him to strip the borrowed T-shirt from her, just as she allowed her to remove his pyjamas.

She discovered that Hugo was a generous lover, arousing her with his hands and his mouth until she was breathless, and then pushing her further until she climaxed and shattered in his arms.

Afterwards, he drew her close, so her head was resting on his shoulder and her arm was wrapped round him.

When she was finally able to collect her thoughts, she said, 'Thank you. But this isn't fair. You're…' Left on the edge, unfulfilled, while she was languorous and sated.

He kissed her lightly. 'It's fine. Next time. And in the meantime I'm going to do complicated equations in my head. Go to sleep, my lark.'

'This feels horribly selfish.'

'Tomorrow,' he said, 'you can make it up to me. Any way you please.'

Which put all sorts of pictures in her head. 'Tomorrow,' she promised.

The warmth of his skin against hers and the darkness of the room pushed her swiftly into sleep.

Hugo lay awake when Alice had turned onto her side, spooned against her. Part of him felt guilty; even though he'd made his peace with Emma, this was the first time he'd made love with someone since she'd gone. And it was weird to be sharing his space again instead of lying there, thinking how big and empty the bed felt. Weird, but comforting as well.

Even though he hadn't reached his own release, he was glad Alice had agreed to stay. He'd enjoyed touching her, the way she'd responded to him.

He liked Alice, full stop. More than liked her. If he was honest with himself, he was halfway to falling in love with her. Since she'd burst into his life, as brightly as one of her butterflies, he'd felt lighter of spirit than he had for years. Instead of just existing, he was connecting with the world again. And it felt really, really good.

He had a feeling that someone had hurt her badly in the past; she'd said her exes had wanted to change her. But maybe he could help her past that, the way she was helping him to move for-

ward again. Maybe she'd trust him and open up
enough to tell him what was holding her back,
and he could help her feel differently about the
situation—make her see just what an amazing
woman she was.

The next morning, Alice woke, slightly disorien-
tated; then she remembered the previous night.

She was in Hugo's bed.

And he was spooned against her, his arm
wrapped round her waist.

She started to twist round and was about to
wake him with a kiss, when he murmured, 'Go
back to sleep, Emma.'

Emma.

He thought she was Emma.

She swallowed hard. Whatever Hugo had said
about wanting to move on, subconsciously he
clearly wasn't ready. He was still in love with
his late wife; and Alice was making a huge mistake, letting herself fall for an unavailable man.
Not one who wanted to change her, this time, but
one who wished she were someone else.

And it hurt so much. She'd tried to resist him
but over the last few days she'd let herself fall
for him. She'd let herself believe that this time
love would work out for her; but she'd been so
very, very wrong. This wasn't like Barney and
his callousness—Hugo wasn't the sort to ride

roughshod over other people—but if anything it hurt more because she knew she could never be what Hugo really wanted. She wasn't the woman he'd loved for most of his adult life. She wasn't *enough*.

How was she going to deal with this?

The first thing she needed to do was to collect her clothes, get dressed, and leave Hugo's house before he woke. Give herself some space to think and work out what to say, so she didn't hurt him: but she knew she couldn't be with him until he was *really* ready to move on.

Given that he wasn't a morning person, she hoped that also meant he was a heavy sleeper.

Tentatively, she wriggled out of his arms, then climbed out of the bed. His discarded T-shirt— the one he'd peeled off her, the night before—was on the floor. She slipped it on, took her phone off charge, and managed to tiptoe downstairs without waking him. Once she'd retrieved her clothes from his washer-dryer, she dressed swiftly and wrote him a note, which she propped against his coffee machine.

Had an early meeting.
Will return your T-shirt later.
A

And then she quietly let herself out of his house.

* * *

Hugo woke when his alarm shrilled; and then he realised something was wrong.

Alice wasn't beside him.

Had he dreamed last night?

No, because the pillow was rumpled.

Tentatively, he slid his arm across her side of the bed. The sheet was cold, so clearly she'd been gone for a while.

Maybe she was downstairs and had just let him sleep in? After all, she was a lark.

But, when he went downstairs, he discovered that the house was empty.

There was a note propped against his coffee machine. He read it and frowned. It was very businesslike and left him feeling that something had gone very wrong between himself and Alice, but he had no idea what or why.

He tried calling her, but her phone went to voicemail. Maybe she really was in a meeting and it hadn't been a polite excuse. But, when she didn't reply to his message by lunchtime he texted her.

Busy tonight? Think Kit and Jenny are free for our celebratory dinner, if Ruth and Andy are?

The reply came within five minutes.

Sorry, can't. Have a departmental thing tonight.

That definitely felt like an excuse. She hadn't mentioned anything to him about a departmental thing yesterday, when they'd talked about celebrating the planning decision.

He decided to ask her outright.

Is everything OK? Have I done something to upset you?

Instead of texting back, she called him. 'Hi.'

'Are you OK?' he asked.

'Yes. Are you?'

But she sounded distant. Polite. 'What's wrong?' he asked.

She sighed. 'You and me—I think we need to move things back a step.'

What? Last night—he'd felt a real connection with her. He was so sure she'd felt the same. 'Why?'

'Because I don't think you're ready to move on with anyone else, right now,' she said.

But he was. He'd *told* her he was. 'Why?' he asked, confused.

'Because you called me Emma,' she said.

'What?' For a moment, shock paralysed his vocal cords. He swallowed hard. 'I'm sorry. I really didn't mean to do that.' But he didn't remember doing it. 'When?'

'This morning.'

He frowned. 'I didn't speak to you this morning. You were gone before I woke.'

'First thing. When I woke. You were still pretty much asleep.'

'Then how did I...?'

'You told me to go back to sleep. And you called me Emma.'

Her voice was very calm, very even, and he didn't have a clue what was going through her head—though he was pretty sure he'd hurt her. 'I'm sorry,' he said again. 'I didn't mean to do that.'

'I know you didn't. But you called me by her name. That tells me you still haven't fully come to terms with losing her. So I think for now it's better that we stick to being colleagues.'

'Alice, I... This...' She wasn't being fair. She'd said herself that he'd been half asleep. But getting angry about it wasn't going to solve the problem. He needed to prove to her that she'd got this wrong. That he did want her. Yet, right now, she was wary and skittish, and it was important that he didn't push her even further away. He raked a hand through his hair. 'That's not what I want.'

'You're still in love with Emma, which is completely understandable, but it's also not fair to either of us. So it's better for us to be just colleagues.'

No, it wasn't. At all. But she'd really got the wrong end of the stick and he needed time to regroup and work out just how he could convince her of the truth. 'Are we still celebrating the planning decision with Kit and Ruth?'

'Of course.'

And he'd just bet that she'd make sure she was sitting as far away from him as possible at dinner and would make an excuse to leave before everyone else.

'Let me know dates and times,' he said, 'and I'll arrange something.' And work out how to persuade her to give him another chance.

It was Friday night when he finally got to see her again. Just as he'd predicted, she sat as far away from him as possible. And she was really, really quiet. So quiet that Ruth followed him when he went to the bar to order another bottle of wine.

'What's happened between you and Alice? If you've hurt—'

'Yes, I have hurt her,' he cut in, 'and I've apologised. It wasn't intentional. And, actually, it's hurt both of us.'

Ruth frowned. 'What happened?'

'She stayed with me on Monday night. I'm rubbish in the mornings. You don't get any sense out of me until after my second cup of coffee. I called her Emma's name when I was still half asleep and I didn't even realise I'd done it. She told me, later in the day, and called it off between us.' He blew out a breath. 'She says I'm not ready to move on. I *am*. But she doesn't believe me, and I don't know how to fix it.'

Ruth's eyes widened. 'I had no idea.'

'Is that something that's happened to her before? She said something about her exes wanting to change her. Was it someone who wanted to make her into a carbon copy of his ex or something?' He shook his head in frustration. 'Because I don't want to do that. I know she's not Emma. She's herself, and that's just the way I want her. I want my nerdy scientist with her mad hair and her amazing facts and the way she sees the world.'

'Then find a way to tell her,' Ruth said.

'That's the problem,' Hugo pointed out. 'She's avoiding me. She doesn't answer my calls—she just texts me to say she's busy with a departmental thing, and I know it's not true. What do I have to do to get her to talk to me? Dress up as a butterfly?'

Ruth's mouth twitched at the corners. 'That might be fun.'

'But it wouldn't get her to see that I lo—' He stopped mid-word as it hit him.

He loved Alice.

And it felt as if he'd just fallen off a cliff, because he didn't know how she felt about him. Only that she'd backed away, which made him think that maybe she didn't feel the same way as him.

'That you…?' Ruth prompted.

He shook his head. 'Sorry to be rude, but it's something I want to talk to her about before I talk to anyone else.' And that was the problem. Getting her to talk to him. 'But I need to find a way to persuade her to talk to me.'

'For what it's worth,' Ruth said, 'I think you're good for each other. She's blossomed since she's been with you.'

'Thank you. I think. But I need more practical help, Ruth. I need to find out what really worries her, so I can talk it through with her and find a solution that works.' He looked at her. 'I won't ask you to break her confidence, and to be honest I think she needs to tell me herself. Can you get her to talk to me?'

'I don't know,' Ruth admitted. 'You need the equivalent of nectar guides.'

Nectar guides. The thing that attracted butterflies.

Alice wasn't a butterfly, but there was something to do with butterflies that he knew—at least, *hoped*—would attract her and get her to talk to him. 'Of course. You're a genius.' He hugged her. 'Thank you.'

'What are you going to do?' Ruth asked.

'Arrange nectar guides,' he said. At her mystified expression, he added, 'I'll explain later.'

Alice was quietly polite for the rest of the evening, and Hugo excused himself early. As soon as he was out of earshot, he rang his mother.

'Ma, where can I buy nettle seeds?'

'Nettle seeds?' Serena sounded surprised. 'I have no idea. Who would want to buy nettle seeds?'

He did. Desperately. 'If I can't get seeds, where can I get the plants?'

'Why?'

He explained the situation and what he planned to do.

'That's *incredibly* romantic,' she said. 'Leave it with me and I'll talk to Jacob. Come down tomorrow for lunch and I'll have it sorted.'

'Thanks, Ma.' He paused. 'She's important to me.'

'I know. For what it's worth, I think this is your best shot. If your father did something like that for me…'

'Too much info, Ma,' he said, smiling. 'I love you. See you tomorrow.'

The next morning, he headed for Sussex. Last time he'd driven this way, he'd spent the day walking hand in hand with Alice on the Downs and on the beach. He'd kissed her. He'd introduced her to the people he loved most in the world, and they'd liked her. The sun had been shining, and life had felt so full of promise.

Today, it was raining. And that was oh, so appropriate.

Jacob was at the house when he arrived.

'You can buy nettle seeds,' he said. 'They take fourteen days to germinate.'

'I can't wait that long,' Hugo said.

'So your ma told me. And there are no nettles in *this* garden.'

Hugo dug his nails into his palm to contain his impatience. 'So where do I get them?'

'I've got friends at the allotments who can't stay on top of their weeds. If you want to come and take them, you're welcome.'

'We prepared seed trays for them this morning,' Serena said. 'So you'll need to put the back seat down for them.'

'Thanks, Ma.'

Hugo spent the day down at the allotments just outside the village, in the rain, weeding patches under Jacob's watchful eye and transferring small nettle plants into the seed trays. Jacob donated his second-best garden fork, spade and trowel and gave him precise instructions on how to make a flowerbed and transfer the nettles. 'I still think you're crazy, mind. Any normal person would do that with flowers. Bedding plants.'

'Trust me, she'd prefer these to bedding plants,' Hugo said.

Sunday was also pouring with rain. Hugo really didn't enjoy digging up a large corner of his lawn, or planting the tiny nettles. He was cold, wet and grumpy by the time he'd finished. And it really wasn't butterfly weather. And it didn't look quite as good as he'd hoped. In the end, he took a photograph from his bedroom window. At least from there you could see the message.

Maybe he'd miscalculated this. Big time.

Especially as now he had to talk Alice into coming here to see it. What if she said no? Then, he decided, he'd have to cheat massively and tell her it was a group thing—and swear Ruth, Andy, Kit and Jenny to secrecy and ask them to turn up an hour later than her, to give him enough time to talk to her.

A hot bath and two mugs of tea did nothing to improve his mood.

What if this wasn't enough?

What if she didn't believe him?

He was about to text her to suggest meeting up when his doorbell rang. He shoved the phone in his pocket and quelled the hope that it might be Alice. Of course it wouldn't be Alice.

James, a friend from his university days who'd

qualified as a surveyor and had promised to survey Rosemary's house for nothing as a donation towards the project, was standing there. 'Sorry, Hugo, I know it's a Sunday, but I thought you'd want to know the results of the survey.'

From the expression on his friend's face, it wasn't good news. 'Come in,' he said. 'Tea, coffee or a beer?'

'Coffee, please. Though you might need gin,' James warned, and proceeded to deliver the bad news.

When James had left, Hugo called Pavani. 'Sorry to be pushy, Pav, and I know it's Sunday, but we've got a problem with the house that means we need money. Have you heard back from any of the potential sponsors?' he asked.

'I'm glad you called—yes, I have,' Pavani said. 'Something came in on Friday, and I've only just had the chance to look at what they said. I'll send the details over now so you can take a look. I can set up a meeting for whenever works for you.'

'Thank you. You're wonderful,' he said.

And then he made the call he'd intended to make, except for very different reasons.

It went straight to voicemail; he sighed inwardly. 'Alice, it's Hugo. I need to talk to you about Rosemary's house. We have good news and bad news, but we definitely need to discuss it. Please call me when you're free.'

Half an hour later, she rang. 'Hi. Sorry I didn't pick up your call earlier. What's happened?'

'Good news or bad, first?'

'Bad,' she said.

'The house has subsidence. James did the survey this morning; he hasn't written it up yet, but he came to tell me what he'd found. It's going to take time—and extra money—to fix.'

'There isn't any spare money,' she said. 'We've already allocated everything I crowdfunded and some of the grants won't come through for months.'

'That's where the good news comes in. Pav said she's found us a sponsor and she's sending the details. Would you mind coming over so we can talk about how we move forward?'

She paused for so long that he thought she was going to say no. 'OK,' she said finally. 'I'll come over now.'

CHAPTER TEN

HUGO'S HOUSE. THE place where the dreams Alice had hardly dared admit to herself had popped, empty as a bubble.

But they needed each other to finalise the butterfly house project. And right now they needed to agree on a plan to move forward with Rosemary's house.

She took the Tube over to Battersea and knocked on his door.

There were dark shadows under his eyes when he opened the door, and she felt guilty; had she done this to him, shoved him back into the shadows where he'd been for the last three years? Then again, she'd been selfish in dragging him into the light when he wasn't really ready.

This was such a mess.

He looked as miserable as she felt. She wanted to put her arms round him and tell him everything was going to be all right; but right now she didn't know if everything would be all right.

'Thanks for coming,' he said.

'You're welcome.' And how horrible it was,

being reduced to formality with him. Though this was her own doing. She'd been the one to walk away.

'Coffee?'

It would be rude to refuse; plus it might help distract her from his nearness. Give her something to do with her hands. 'Thank you.'

Once she was sitting at the table with a mug of coffee, he showed her the file James had given him. 'It's quite bad. The house needs underpinning. Although the house insurance will cover repairing the damage, it won't cover preventing future subsidence.'

She looked at James's figures and winced. 'We don't have that sort of money.'

'Which is where Pav's sponsor comes in. Apparently it's a firm of stockbrokers who want to showcase their green credentials, and they think sponsoring us will help them do that. They get their name on our website and a "sponsored by" board in our reception area, and Pav's suggested holding a special event once a quarter for their clients. I think we should accept.'

'OK. So who are they?'

He opened the file Pav had sent over.

Alice looked at it, and her vision blurred.

Rutherford and Associates, Stockbrokers
Managing partner: Barney Rutherford

No.

It couldn't be.

She took a deep breath to calm herself. When she thought about it rationally, Barney wasn't an uncommon first name and Rutherford wasn't an uncommon surname.

All the same…

'Can I just check something?' she asked, picking up her phone.

'Sure.'

She quickly flicked into the firm's website, and clicked on the 'about us' section.

And there he was. Barney Rutherford. Expensive suit, handmade shirt, silk tie. Probably the same kind of shoes that Hugo wore. A little fatter, a little less hair, but still recognisable as the man who'd hurt her so much all those years ago.

'No,' she said.

Hugo frowned. 'Sorry?'

'No. We're not taking that man's money. We'll have to find another way.'

His frown deepened. 'I don't understand. Do you know him or something?'

'Yes, and he has no moral compass whatsoever. He's not having anything to do with the butterfly house.'

'He's offering us enough to fix the house. Otherwise we might be held up for months and months.'

'I don't care.' Anger she'd suppressed for all these years felt as if it was bursting through her. 'We're not taking his money.'

'OK,' Hugo said carefully. 'But, as I can't see the problem, would you mind telling me why?'

She stared into her coffee. 'He was at Oxford when I was there. I hated my first year. Maybe I picked the wrong college, but I didn't fit in. I was the granddaughter of a coal miner and I had a funny accent. I came from a council estate instead of a country estate. I didn't go to a posh school.' She grimaced and shook her head. 'So I just got on with my work, and showed my face where I had to, but social situations were horrible. There were all these invisible tests I kept failing.

'I told myself it would be better in the second year, but it wasn't. And then Barney came up to me one day in the library. He said he'd noticed me in the quad. He wanted to go out with me. I thought it was probably some sort of joke, so I said no. But he persisted, and eventually I agreed.' She looked up at Hugo. 'And it was amazing. He made me feel as if I was special. All these girls from his background were just queuing up to date him, but he'd chosen *me*. I didn't like the people he mixed with very much, but he kind of protected me from them, and he taught me all the little social things that never occurred to me. He got me to change the way I wore my hair, the way I dressed, so I fitted in.'

It was all horribly clear to Hugo, now. He understood why Alice had been twitchy about meeting his parents, about wearing the right things. Especially as it sounded as if his background was similar to Barney's. She must've been terrified that they'd find her lacking.

'You didn't need to change who you were,' he said softly. 'There's nothing wrong with you at all.'

'I changed,' she said. 'I fitted in. And it was wonderful. I'd never been happier. I adored Barney. I really thought he was the one, and he dropped so many hints that I thought he was going to ask me to marry him at the Commemoration Ball. I got this really special dress. I actually used my overdraft, because I wanted it to be special in case he really did propose—it was something I wanted to remember for ever. It started out as the perfect evening, and even the bitchier girls in his set were nice to me.'

Hugo had a feeling that there was a 'but' coming. A seriously nasty 'but'.

'And then I overhead them talking in the toilets. They didn't know I was there. They were saying how Barney was going to win his bet; he was going to win a lot of money from his pals, that night, because he'd managed to turn the oik into one of them. I couldn't believe it. I honestly thought he loved me—but it turned out that he was mocking me as much as the others did. He was only going out with me for a bet. It was a weird kind of Eliza Doolittle thing. Make the girl from t'pit into a toff.'

She dragged in a breath. 'When I walked out of the toilet and washed my hands, the other girls were still there and they looked horrified. I could see them mouthing frantically to each other, wondering if I'd overheard. I just ignored them and walked back into the ballroom. Barney was talking to his friends and he didn't see me come up behind him. But I heard what they said. It was all "tonight's the night". Earlier, I would've thought that they knew he was going to propose to me, but after what I'd just heard I knew it had a different meaning.'

Hugo was shocked by how unkind Barney and his friends had been, but he wasn't going to interrupt Alice now. She needed to get this out of her head, once and for all.

'I asked Barney to come outside with me—I wasn't going to have this conversation in front of his mates. Then I said I'd heard that he was dating me for a bet. He blustered, but I could see the truth in his eyes. I asked him if tonight was the deadline for his bet. And then he said yes. I asked how much he was going to win. He wouldn't tell me, and I said if he had a shred of decency he'd donate that money to a shelter for the homeless. That I never wanted to see him again. And then I walked out.' She bit her lip. 'I felt so stupid. So used. I thought he loved me. And all along I'd just been a joke to him. Free sex, because I was stupid enough to think he mattered and I gave him my virginity—and no doubt he boasted about *that* to all his mates, too.' She shrugged.

'The last week of term was awful. Everyone was laughing at me, at how stupid I'd been to think that someone like Barney Rutherford would ever be serious about someone like me. I thought about just leaving Oxford so I didn't have to face any of them again, but that would've meant they'd won. So instead I went to see my personal tutor and asked if I could move college. I said it was awkward because I'd split up with Barney, and I wanted to concentrate on my studies and not get distracted by anything else. My tutor was lovely and told me to stay at college, and he helped me find somewhere else to live for the third year. I didn't socialise much in my last year, just focused on my work.' She lifted her chin. 'I graduated top of my year and scooped a couple of awards. But best of all I got my place to do my MA and then my PhD in London. And it was a lot better—people actually liked me for myself, here. It didn't matter where I came from.' She dragged in a breath. 'And that is why I'm not taking *any-thing* from Barney Rutherford.'

He took her hand. 'First off, that was a really horrible thing to do to you. I don't understand the kind of man who'd behave like that, and you really didn't deserve to be treated like that. Secondly, I think you're amazing because you rose above it all and didn't let them drive you out.'

'But did I?' she asked. 'I seem to be completely useless at picking Mr Right. Every man I've dated since then—well, except you—has wanted to change me. It always starts off all right, but then he wants me to dress differently or do my hair differently or speak differently, or do something more girly and less scientific, or...' She shook her head. 'I think there's something wrong with me. I can't move on from being the oik who doesn't quite fit in.'

'You're not an oik,' he said.

'No? Barney and his lot were right. Appearances matter.'

'Only on a very superficial level,' he said.

'Come off it, Hugo. Look at your industry. It's about beautiful buildings.'

'But if they're beautiful and don't do their job, they're a failure,' he pointed out.

'Everyone dresses in posh suits.'

'It's a convention,' he said. 'Though, actually, if you're a really brilliant architect, you can wear odd socks and crumpled clothes and everyone will just think you're quirky.'

'Even if you've got the wrong accent and the wrong background?'

'There's no such thing as a wrong accent and a wrong background. It's what you do that matters,' he said. 'What's in your head and what's in your heart.'

Why couldn't she believe him? Why couldn't she move on?

'But even you,' she said. 'You wanted me to be something different.'

He shook his head. 'I've never asked you to change the way you dress. Actually, I happen to *like* the way you dress. You're incredibly cute. Especially with those sassy slogans on your T-shirts.'

'I don't mean that.' She looked away. 'That morning... I was so happy, when I woke in your arms. And then you called me Emma, and I knew it wasn't me you really wanted. You wanted her. And I can't be her. I just can't.'

His intake of breath was audible, and she winced. 'Sorry. I didn't mean that to sound as bad as it did.'

'It sounded bad,' he said, 'and it *is* bad, because it's not fair. Other than Emma, you're the first woman I've slept with in more than a decade. And you know I'm an owl, Alice. You can't even talk to me until I've had two cups of coffee in the morning, because I'm so not a morning person and what comes out of my mouth won't make any sense. Yes, I miss my wife. I loved her so much and we were happy together. But she *died*, Alice. She's not here any more and nobody can bring her back. She wouldn't want me to spend the rest of my life, alone and grieving—though that was exactly what I was doing until I met you. And then you started changing things. You changed the way I see things, showed me that there's still light in the world and I need to stop trudging along in my lonely little rut and reach for the sunlight. You showed me there are butterflies. That I can stop existing with boxes around me, that putting flowers everywhere makes life better.'

He stood up. 'Come with me. There's something I need to show you. And I don't care that it's raining and I don't care if you trudge mud all over my floor—or—' He waved one hand in seeming exasperation, clearly failing to find the right words. 'Oh, just come with me, Alice. Please.'

She followed him out into the garden. And then she saw what she hadn't noticed when she'd walked into his house: that the right-hand far corner of the garden wasn't a neat manicured lawn any more. He'd dug a flower bed.

'It's a flower bed,' she said.

'No. No, it isn't.' He shook his head and took her hand. 'Look closer.'

She walked across the lawn with him, and then she realised.

He'd planted *nettles*.

'You're making a wild corner.'

'It's a nectar guide. An Alice guide,' he said. 'And I got it wrong because you can't see it properly at this angle. You need to see it from my bedroom window—and I don't want to tell you to go upstairs and look at it because I don't want you to get the wrong idea.' He pulled his phone from his pocket, flicked into the photo app and selected a photo. 'Here.'

She stared at it.

The flower bed contained a heart shape. And written in nettles were the words *Hugo Loves Alice*.

'You love me,' she said in wonder.

'Yes. I love you enough to change my garden for you—and do you have any idea how hard it is to find baby nettles?'

'How did you do it?' she asked.

'I spent the whole of yesterday digging various people's allotments and taking out weeds—in the rain, and just so you know I refused to move the thistles on the ground that they're important butterfly food sources—in exchange for baby nettles,' he said. 'I brought them back from Sussex in seed trays donated by my mother. And I spent the whole of today using Jacob's second-best spade, fork and trowel to make a proper bed for them and planting them. In the rain. Because I didn't know how else to tell you how I feel.'

'You love me,' she said again, not quite taking it in.

'Yes. I love the real you. The scientist who sends me nerdy facts and teases me about my shoes and worries about ticks. The woman who has slogans on her T-shirt and mad hair. The woman who sees beauty and teaches other people how to see it, too. You're like those Morphos you showed me at the butterfly house—all quiet and hiding in the background, like they are when their wings are closed. And then you start talking about your subject, and you open up, and you're stunning—just like a Morpho flying. I can't take my eyes off you. And I'm not saying that because I've got any hidden agendas. I love you and I want to be with you. I know I messed it up and I hurt you, and I'm sorry. But I really do love you, Alice.'

'I'm sorry, too,' she said. 'I let my past get in the way. I didn't give you a chance to explain. I thought I knew best—and I don't.'

'I'm glad you realise that,' he said. 'Because I think we've got a future. Just we both need to compromise a bit.'

'Yes.' She looked at him. 'I love you, too, Hugo. Even though you're posh and you're a walking clothes horse, you're… You've shown me things, too. Beautiful structures, the way the light gets in. The way you feel about glass and staircases, that's like the way I feel about butterflies. You get me, and I get you. And I hurt you as much as you hurt me, by being proud and stubborn and too scared to take a chance on you. I'm sorry.'

'We're both going to have to work on communication, in the future,' he said. 'But, for now…' He cupped her face in his hand, dipped his head and kissed her. 'I love you,' he whispered. 'And now I think we'd better go back inside before we're both completely soaked.'

Once he'd closed the glass door behind them, he drew her back into his arms. 'If you don't want to take Barney's money, that's fine. We'll find another sponsor.'

She kissed him. 'Why do I feel there's a "but"?'

'Because there is one,' he said. 'He hurt you. He owes you a massive apology. And we could make something good happen out of something bad.'

'How?'

'Take the money. Except *you'll* be the one to take it and make very sure he knows who you are. And that you've won, because you're the one who's made a real difference to the world—to your students, to the butterflies, and to me.'

Could she?

Should she?

'Think about it,' he said. 'I'm here if you want to bounce ideas. Whatever you decide, that won't change how I feel about you. I love you; my family and my best friend think you're wonderful; and I maybe need to work a little harder until you think I'm good enough to meet your family.'

'You're good enough,' she said. 'I think they'll see you the same way Ruth does. And she thinks you're fabulous, by the way.'

'Good,' he said. 'So we get to start again?'

She shook her head. 'We don't need to start again. You were right the first time. We just need to communicate a bit better in future.'

'So was Jacob right and I should've written that message in proper flowers?'

She laughed. 'No. You were right to say it with nettles. Give my butterflies somewhere to lay their eggs and for their caterpillars to feed. It's the most romantic thing I've ever, ever seen.'

'You,' he said, 'are *weird*.'

She grinned. 'Takes one to know one…'

Two days later, Alice headed to Rutherford and Associates, walking hand in hand with Hugo, wearing her favourite T-shirt and jeans and hiking boots.

'That looks like battle gear,' Hugo said.

'It is,' she said. 'I don't need to dress up or have a posh accent; it's who I am and what I can do that's really important. I'm a butterfly specialist— so I'm going to look like one.'

'You've missed a few words out, Dr Walters,' he said. 'You're also brilliant, brave and generally fantastic.' He kissed her lightly. 'I'm going to loiter in the coffee shop across the road. Call me if you need me—but I don't think you will. You're more than good enough on your own, just as you are.'

Ten years ago, she wouldn't have believed him. Maybe even earlier in the summer she wouldn't have been sure. But now, she knew he was right. She was good enough, just as she was.

She took a deep breath. 'I'll come and find you when I'm done.'

Five minutes later, she was in Barney's office.

'Thank you for coming to talk about the project, Dr Walters.' Then he peered at her. *Alice?*'

She inclined her head. 'You remember me?'

His face suffused with colour. 'Yes.'

'The oik. Your Yorkshire version of Eliza Doolittle.' She made her accent that little bit broader. 'But it isn't what you look like or what you sound like that matters, Barney. It's who you are. How you treat other people. How you behave.'

He stared at her.

'It's all right. I'm not going to start a fight. I don't expect you to apologise.' She looked at him. 'I don't need your approval or your apologies, because I already have the respect of people who actually matter.'

'So why are you here?' he asked.

'Because,' she said, 'you offered sponsorship for the butterfly house. And I'm looking at this purely as a business transaction. Yes, I could take the moral high ground and refuse your money— but then we'd have to find another sponsor, and I'd rather spend my time on other things. So I'm here to accept your money. And I wanted to do it in person so you know I'm not intimidated by you or your family or your friends—not the way I was at Oxford.'

He looked at her. 'I wasn't very nice to you.'

'No, you weren't,' she agreed.

'I didn't know you were involved in this project.'

'Does that mean you're withdrawing your offer?'

He gave her a wry smile. 'No. It doesn't. Please, take a seat.'

She did so. 'So why did you offer us the sponsorship?'

'My clients want green investments, so it makes sense for us to sponsor something involving ecology,' he said.

'Why the butterfly house?'

'Because I have a daughter. Daisy's four years old and she loves butterflies,' he said. 'I wanted to do something for her, too, something she could be proud of when she grows up.'

So maybe Barney had changed.

He shifted in his seat. 'When she's older, if anyone treats her the way I treated you at Oxford, I'll want to tear him apart with my bare hands. I know you said you didn't want an apology, but you deserve one.' He took a deep breath. 'I'm sorry, Alice. I'm not who I was back then, either. I hope I've grown up, become a better person.'

She hoped so, too.

'I'll match my company's sponsorship personally. In the circumstances, that's the least I can do.'

She hadn't expected that. 'Thank you. Obviously you've had the information from our PR people, but I think you need to know exactly what we're doing.' And she talked him through the project, everything from Viola's work through to Rosemary's, to the design Hugo had made for the butterfly house and the kind of educational resources they were going to offer. As she talked, her confidence grew. And she wasn't The Oik any more. She was Dr Alice Walters. Professional. Good at what she did.

'That,' Barney said when she'd finished, 'sounds amazing. My clients are going to be thrilled.' He smiled. 'And so is my daughter.'

Alice knew she could walk away now, triumphant. Or she could do something better: she could build a bridge. 'We're re-wilding the garden over the summer as well as building the butterfly house. Bring your daughter to see us, with her mum. She can help to plant something, and then she'll always know that she helped make a difference to that little corner of the garden.'

'I'd like that,' he said. 'Thank you, Alice.'

She stood up, and reached across the desk to shake his hand, knowing that finally she had closure on her past. 'You're welcome. And thank you for sponsoring our project. You're helping to make a difference.'

Then she walked over to the coffee shop to meet Hugo.

'Are you OK?' he asked when she sat down opposite him.

She nodded. 'I faced him. I wasn't sure if I was more angry or worried that he wouldn't take me seriously—but then I realised that you were right. I make a difference. It's not just what I do at work, it's who I am as well.' She smiled. 'And he apologised.'

'Good. That was long overdue.' He leaned over and took her hands. 'And I'm guessing he's going to give us the money Pav asked for and a bit more.'

She looked at him, shocked. 'How did you know?'

'Because you, my love, were going to talk to him about the project. And when you talk about butterflies, you sparkle and you light up the room. You're amazing and you're irresistible.'

Hugo valued her for who she was. Loved her for who she was. And that made her hold her head that little bit higher. Finally, she'd moved on from being the oik Barney's set had laughed at. She was herself. She was *enough*.

'We don't have to accept his money,' Hugo said, when she didn't say anything. 'This is your project. You make the call.'

'It's your project too. And Rosemary's, Viola's and Emma's. It's teamwork.'

'But you,' Hugo said, 'are my priority.'

And how amazing that made her feel. He was putting her first. 'We'll accept it,' she said. 'Because this gorgeous architect I happen to know taught me the value of building things with good foundations. His daughter likes butterflies. I told him to bring her to the house and she can help plant something.'

'Great idea.' He inclined his head. 'Congratulations on nailing the deal.'

'With your support.'

'I didn't do anything.' He shrugged. 'I just sat here, drinking coffee.'

'You were here as my backup if I needed you.' She stole a kiss. 'You believed in me. More than that, you've taught me that I'm OK with who I am.'

'My brilliant, gorgeous butterfly specialist.' He kissed her back. 'I love you. And I can't wait for the future.'

'My brilliant, gorgeous architect. I love you, too. And we're going to build the butterfly house. Fulfil Rosemary's dream.'

'And,' he said softly, 'our own. You, me and the future.'

'You, me and the future,' she echoed.

EPILOGUE

A year later

'I WONDER WHY Philip Hemingford wants to see us in his office,' Hugo asked Alice as they walked through Chelsea together.

'Last time we had an appointment with him, he practically had to referee a fight,' Alice said. 'When you thought I was a gold-digger.'

'And you thought I was a vain clothes horse.'

She looked pointedly at his shoes. 'Says the man with handmade Italian stuff on his feet.'

He laughed, and kissed her. 'And who was it who found me that suit on our honeymoon, Dr Grey?'

'You looked cute in it,' she said with a grin.

Hand in hand, they walked into the solicitor's office. He was already waiting for them.

'Lovely to see you both,' he said, shaking their hands in turn. 'Thank you for the invitation to the opening of the butterfly house next week. I'm looking forward to it.'

'Pleasure,' Alice said.

'So what can we do for you?' Hugo asked.

'I have a letter from Miss Grey. You've met the conditions for it to be given to you,' he said.

'A letter from Great-Aunt Rosemary? For both of us?' Hugo looked confused.

'Yes.'

'Do you have any idea what's in it?' she asked.

He shook his head. 'None at all. Miss Grey was a bit of a law unto herself.'

'Perhaps we should ask you to read it to us,' Hugo said. 'And we promise not to shout at each other.'

The solicitor gave a small smile. 'I'm glad to hear that.' He opened the letter and scanned it.

'What does she say?' Alice asked impatiently.

My dear Hugo and Alice,
If you're reading this, then I know my dearest wish has come true. I've been trying to get you to meet each other for months, but whenever one of you was at the house with me the other one wasn't.

The only way I could think of to get you to meet was to change my will. I knew you'd have to be at the solicitor's, and I hoped that if you worked together—with you in charge of the garden and the butterflies, Alice, and you in charge of the buildings, Hugo—you'd see the same that I do. That you're perfect for each other.

I know you've both suffered a lot in the past, and I think you'll make each other very happy.

Congratulations on your wedding, and I do hope you'll forgive an old woman for interfering.

With much love to you both,
Rosemary

Hugo and Alice looked at each other.

'Matchmaking from beyond the grave,' Hugo said.

'And she was right. We're perfect for each other,' Alice said. 'If she hadn't changed her will and put in those conditions, we probably wouldn't have met.'

'We wouldn't be married,' he said.

She rested her hand on the almost imperceptible bump of her stomach. 'I have a feeling that this little one's going to be a girl. And I also think her name should be Rosemary Viola Emma Grey.'

'Rosemary Viola Emma Grey,' Hugo echoed, and his eyes were full of love.

* * * * *

If you enjoyed this story,
check out these other great reads from
Kate Hardy

One Night to Remember
Soldier Prince's Secret Baby Gift
Finding Mr. Right in Florence
A Diamond in the Snow

All available now!